She wanted more

"Please..." Paris could manage only one word, but that was all it took. He pulled her to him and his mouth claimed hers, his tongue challenging hers in the timeless battle of male against female, lust against desire. She writhed against him, wanting a satisfaction his kisses alone wouldn't bring.

He released his claim on her mouth. "You're killing me. I can't keep kissing you, touching you, and not be deep inside you." His voice was raw with desire. "Paris, what do you want?"

Her eyes locked with his, knowing that if he could see into her heart, he would see the passion. For years, she'd only known adventure through her books. For one night, she wanted to live that adventure. With him. With Alexander.

"You," she whispered. "Tonight, I want you." Maybe it was crazy, but tonight, with a desperation she'd never felt before, she wanted him inside her. It didn't matter that he couldn't really be Alexander. Hadn't he told her that, just for tonight, he was? And he had to be...

He had to be her dream man. After all, who besides Alexander could make her feel this way?

W9-AUK-025

Dear Reader,

Temptation men. Larger-than-life, sexy, caring men who make your heart pick up tempo. Men that any woman would welcome into her heart and into her bed. But what would you do if one of these men actually came to life? That's the idea behind *Nobody Does It Better,* my first Temptation title. And, of course, there's a twist.

Paris has found her dream man in Montgomery Alexander. The problem? *Alexander doesn't exist.* She created him as a pseudonym for the pulse-pounding spy novels she writes. Devin O'Malley's a sexy-as-sin entrepreneur with a shady past. And he needs cash fast! So when he overhears Paris's secret and realizes her publisher expects Alexander to show up for a party...well, what's a guy to do?

Fantasy, fun, romance. Isn't that what Temptation is all about? I hope you enjoy reading about Devin and Paris's romance. I assure you, it's a sensual one!

Enjoy,

Julie Kenner

P.S. I'd love to hear from you. You can write to me at P.O. Box 151417, Austin, TX 78715-1417, or e-mail me at jkenner@sig.net.

P.P.S. Rachel isn't one to put up with being a secondary character for long. So don't be surprised if she graces the pages of another Temptation novel—as soon as I can come up with a hero who can handle her!

NOBODY DOES IT BETTER
Julie Kenner

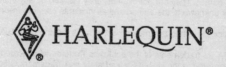

HARLEQUIN®

TORONTO • NEW YORK • LONDON
AMSTERDAM • PARIS • SYDNEY • HAMBURG
STOCKHOLM • ATHENS • TOKYO • MILAN • MADRID
PRAGUE • WARSAW • BUDAPEST • AUCKLAND

This book is dedicated to all the people who provided that little bit of magic it takes to coax a story to make the leap from imagination to paper. Especially my husband, Don, for being there, and my mom, Anna, for everything. Extra thanks to Kathleen, for her support and input every step of the way, and for indulging my caffeine addiction in the process. Latte, anyone? To Dee, for joining us and rounding out one heck of a group. And to my wonderful editor, Brenda Chin, whose support and encouragement have meant so much. Thanks for never letting me doubt it would happen, and for bringing me into the Harlequin family.

ISBN 0-373-25872-0

NOBODY DOES IT BETTER

Copyright © 2000 by Julie Beck Kenner.

Printed in U.S.A.

1

"YOU NEED A MAN."

"Rachel!" Paris Sommers choked on her wine and scrunched lower into the booth. She would have preferred a quiet slide into oblivion, but since that wasn't possible, poor posture would have to suffice.

"I'm serious," Rachel continued. "All we need to do is find you an able-bodied male. You use him for one night. Bingo. Problem solved. Just pick one, already."

Paris scanned the dimly lit Irish pub nestled in the heart of Manhattan. Thankfully, most of the patrons seemed uninterested, studying their pints instead. Some looked up, but then laconically turned away. Only a nearby waiter seemed even the slightest bit intrigued, and Paris caught his eye before he turned back to gathering dirty glasses from an adjacent table.

Pulling herself up, Paris leaned over the polished table-top until she was nose to nose with Rachel. "Let's lay off the men talk, okay?" She cast a meaningful glance toward the waiter. "People might misunderstand."

"Afraid he'll think you're looking to get laid?"

"Stop it," hissed Paris, knowing he must have overheard. Sure enough, his head tilted just a little so he could watch them. Despite the shadows, Paris swore she saw the hint of a smirk playing at the corner of his mouth as he moved away to wipe down another table.

The muted lighting prevented her from getting a good

look at him, but what she could see, she liked. Strong features, a nice smile and just a hint of charisma. Well, that figured. A gorgeous guy looks her way and she's having a ridiculous conversation about getting laid.

She frowned. Rachel Dean might have been her best friend since kindergarten, and her literary agent for the past six years, but she could still be a royal pain.

"Come on, Paris. Half your characters parade around in tiny bikinis on the arms of virile government agents. You'd think I could say 'laid' without you blushing."

"That's why they call it fiction."

"Yet another reason you really do need a man."

"Unlike some people, I have standards."

Rachel pointed to herself and raised her eyebrows. "*Moi?* I have standards. Male. That's a standard."

Paris rolled her eyes. Rachel might not be a saint, but she was still a far cry from the sophisticated, experienced vixen she tried so hard to appear to be. "Maybe so, but the mere existence of a Y-chromosome doesn't do it for me." She wanted more. A lot more.

"No. You want Alexander. What would you do if he walked through that door? You'd jump him and have your wicked way with him right in front of us lawabiding bar patrons."

Paris felt the telltale warmth of a blush creep up the back of her neck. Rachel knew her far too well.

"*Au contraire*, my friend," she said, trying to cover. "I'm much too refined." She pushed her hair out of her eyes and smiled sweetly. "The floor's way too hard."

Rachel downed the last of her beer. "Got news for you, kiddo. It ain't gonna happen. And meantime, your diaphragm's collecting cobwebs."

"Of course it's not happening, because I am *not* waiting for Alexander," Paris insisted, adding a little extra emphasis, more for herself than for Rachel. Hadn't she told herself over and over to let go of the fantasy that someone as delicious as Alexander would suddenly sweep her off her feet?

Trouble was, Alexander was a rare breed, a hard man to give up. Sophisticated, yet witty. Cold as steel to his enemies. Hot as molten lava with his lover. Fiercely loyal, utterly sexy. A man with the poise of a prince and the coolness of an assassin, Alexander could melt a woman's heart with a well-placed look.

Paris closed her eyes and sighed. No matter how much she wanted him next to her, Alexander was not going to miraculously appear. Not in person. Not in the flesh.

Hadn't she dated enough men to know that?

She took another sip of wine, then studied the deep red liquid. It was just as well, really. She knew exactly what she wanted out of life, had it all mapped out, in fact. Alexander was too suave, too cool, too *dangerous* to be part of the respectable suburban life she'd get around to eventually.

She twirled the stem of her wineglass between her fingers. True, there was a part of her—a tiny but persistent part—that prodded her to cut loose, to take a walk on the wild side. To get out there and squeeze the Charmin at least once.

She'd struggled hard to keep that part under control, and she didn't intend to blow it. A man like Alexander would throw a real kink into her carefully thought out plans. So it was for the best that he'd never appeared on her doorstep.

At least, that's what she kept telling herself.

Rachel leaned back in the booth and snorted. "Well, if you're not waiting for an Alexander to sweep you off your feet, then what the devil are you waiting for?"

"Nothing. I date. I date *nice* men, the right kind of men." Men who did absolutely nothing for her. No heart pounding. No toes curling. No...anything.

"The kind Daddy would approve of? Let me give you a clue, my friend. You date boring men. And you don't even do that very often. Actually, considering the men I've seen you go out with, it's just as well your diaphragm's a little dusty."

She glared at Rachel. "For your information, I don't even own one."

"Maybe you should. You need a little adventure in your life."

Paris wasn't about to confess that she'd been thinking almost that very thing. "I have adventure. I'm practically drowning in adventure." What she really wanted was passion. Just one taste of the stomach-churning, knees-wobbling, lose-all-control kind of passion she imagined with Alexander. One moment of reality to fuel her imagination and tide her over for the rest of her life.

"You've got adventure, sure. But it's in your head. I'm talking reality."

"You're talking nonsense," Paris said, more harshly than she intended. "Could we get back on track? I didn't force myself onto a plane, leave my goldfish with a neighbor, and come all the way from Texas for Introduction to Dating 101." She took the last gulp of wine and leaned back, then saw the cute waiter out of the corner of her eye, staring right at her. And soaking up every word.

Great. Just great. When his smirk transformed into a full-blown smile, the heat in her cheeks rose in proportion to his expanding grin. Her stomach lurched as mortification swept over her. Half of her wanted to ask him out just to show Rachel up. Her more practical half wanted to scold him for eavesdropping on a rather embarrassing conversation.

She chose a middle ground. "Could you bring us some water?"

"Sure thing." His deep voice held just enough of a New York accent to add flair without stealing attention from the rest of him. As he leaned over to clear their empty glasses, Paris inhaled his cinnamon-musk scent, a nice contrast to the smell of beer and tobacco that wafted through the pub. The dark stubble on his face contrasted with honey-colored waves to give him a wild, bohemian quality. His hair was the kind a woman's fingers, and her kisses, could get lost in.

His profile danced on the edge of her memory, just inches out of reach. Why did he seem so familiar? She knew she'd never seen him before, yet his appearance called to her. His features were angular, with high cheekbones and a well-defined jawline. The tip of his nose bent just a little, as if broken in a reckless youth.

He moved away, weaving his way through the tables.

Then it hit her—that chiseled face, the sensual mouth, his bad-boy-playing-at-respectable air. Could it really be?

"Waiter!" she called, desperate for another look. When he turned and stepped into the light, Paris quelled a gasp. She'd been right. In her mind, she could picture every line, every angle, every contour of Alexander's face. Except for the dark blond hair, this waiter could be Alexander's twin.

"Miss?"

With a start, she realized she'd been staring, her mouth hanging open like an idiot. At least she'd refrained from drooling.

She grappled for something to say, then noticed the

empty bowl that had earlier held cashews. "Um...could we also get something to nibble on?"

Her cute waiter nodded. "No problem."

DEVIN O'MALLEY TRIED to get a grip on himself. He rarely noticed women. For years he'd been too immersed in his business to bother. Of course, that didn't stop the women from noticing *him*, and if they made the first move, Devin had no qualms about reciprocating. He'd entertained plenty like the brunette named Rachel, in and out of his bed, usually converting their casual talk about sex into low-pitched moans and desperate pleas once the lights went out.

Yet he'd never once experienced such a tug of pleasure just from watching a woman like the petite blonde with the deep brown eyes. And it had been ages since he'd puzzled over how to ask a perfect stranger out on a date.

But he was wondering about how to ask this one.

Paris. The name seemed to fit, even though she lacked the exotic appearance he'd expect to accompany that name. She wasn't a classic beauty. Each of her features, standing alone, boasted some flaw. Brown doe-eyes spaced a little too far apart, untamed eyebrows a shade darker than her neatly pinned golden curls, a nose that was just a little crooked, a too-small mouth that didn't do justice to the perfectly shaped, full lips.

Empirically, her features were flawed. As a whole, her face was striking. It had certainly struck Devin. She was every fantasy he'd ever had rolled into one woman. And then some.

Her friend said she needed a man. Well, he intended to apply for the job.

"Pass me some nuts, would you, Jerry?" Devin asked as he slipped behind the mahogany and brass bar.

"We're out. Want me to run to the back?"

"I'll do it," he said, actually grateful no one had bothered to stock the bar. He needed a few minutes to get his head in order. To plan his attack.

A large room with high ceilings and bare walls, the stockroom was a hodgepodge of electronic gadgetry and miscellaneous supplies. Devin found the cashews under a stack of misprinted menus and grabbed a box.

"Larry? Federal prosecutor Larry? He doesn't have any magnetism. No one will buy that he's Alexander." Devin almost dropped his bundle. That smooth voice belonged to *her*.

"Well, I'll be," he mumbled. He'd forgotten that the room shared a thin wall with booth twelve.

"He's perfectly fine," Rachel replied.

"People have an image of Montgomery Alexander. Not just anyone can step into his shoes."

Whoever this Alexander guy was, Paris sure seemed taken with him. The lucky bastard.

Devin took a deep breath. What the hell was he doing, eavesdropping on a woman he didn't know and envying a man he'd never met? "Dev, you're a basket case," he muttered.

"You can say that again."

Jerry's whisper carried, and Devin spun around, a finger to his lips.

"Don't worry," Jerry assured. "The sound only comes in. Don't ask me why. I just—"

Devin held up his hand. The women were talking again.

"So you're okay with the idea?" Rachel asked. "All we have to do is find the right guy?"

"No, I'm not okay with it." That was Paris. He pictured her with slightly raised eyebrows, like a woman scolding a small child. "Even if he looked perfect, how can we be sure this guy would keep the secret? Besides, it's not right. It'd be like we were scamming everyone."

"Scamming? Honey, what do you think we're doing now?"

"Nothing," Paris insisted. "Montgomery L. Alexander is just a pen name. My pen name."

"Well, I'll be damned," whispered Jerry. "Who woulda thought Montgomery Alexander was a broad?"

The knot in Devin's stomach loosened and his heart picked up its tempo. He caught himself smiling and almost laughed out loud. There was no Alexander. It was just a pseudonym.

His reaction bordered on absurd, and he knew it. She didn't know him from Adam. Just because there was no Alexander didn't mean she was going to rush into Devin's arms and smother him with kisses. So what difference did it make if this Alexander guy was out of the picture? None. Zip. Zilch. Nada.

Didn't matter. The logic center of his brain must have taken a vacation and left the lust department in control. All he could think was that Alexander's untimely demise left one less person in the world to compete with for her attention.

Now he just had to figure out how to *get* her attention.

"Okay," Rachel finally said, and Devin imagined her leaning back into the worn red leather booth, gathering steam for her next attack on Paris's logic. "But there's a drawing of Alexander on the back of your latest book. There've been articles, and web-pages, and on-line interviews. There are even women who swear they've slept with the man. You didn't expect that, and neither did I. But that's what we're dealing with now."

"I should just 'fess up and tell the truth at the party." Paris said, sounding as if she'd prefer to have a root canal.

"And ruin everything? Hardback book deal. Remember? Money, publicity, the whole nine yards. Remember? You know Cobalt Blue's only going to make an offer if Alexander comes through at the party tomorrow."

"I know. I know. Besides, I'm just babbling. You know I can't tell the truth. Not now. I'm in too deep."

"So, let's go out and find us an Alexander." There was a pause. "What? Oh, no. You're not going to say what I think you're going to say."

"But it's true," Paris insisted. "Not just anyone can be Alexander. He's special. He's unique."

"Hello? Anybody home? He's made up. Or are you going mental on me?"

Paris laughed. "Haven't I always been?"

"Well, I'll give you that."

Devin heard shuffling.

"But what about the party?" Rachel asked. "We need time to find the right guy."

"Maybe we could say he missed his plane from London." Although her voice was muffled, Devin could just make out what Paris said. "As his personal manager, I guess little ol' me will just have to break the bad news."

Her voice barely penetrated the wall, and Devin realized they were leaving. The urge to see her again overwhelmed him, and he was on his feet and out the door before the echo faded. He burst into the dining area just as the front door swung shut.

"Damn, damn, damn," he spewed, startling an old man munching pretzels at the bar. Without stopping to consider, he sprinted for the door, opened it and stepped into the heavy August heat. Paris stood across the street, about to slip into a taxi.

For a moment, she seemed to look right at him. Without thinking, he took a step toward her. Her mouth twitched in what could have been a smile, then she ducked in, slammed the door and was gone.

Devin mentally shook himself. He was acting like a flake. Since when did Devin O'Malley run after anonymous women? He tried to laugh it off, blaming his quirky behavior on testosterone, sunspots, or his fast-approaching thirty-first birthday. Anything to lessen the feeling that he had suddenly and without warning lost something terribly important.

"Answer to your prayers, eh, boss?"

"She's a diamond, Jerry," Devin answered, without turning around. "In case you hadn't noticed, I'm coal. My whole family's coal. If I'm lucky, maybe I'll make it to graphite by the next millennium. But not diamonds. Never diamonds." *And that was a damn shame.*

"I ain't suggesting you marry her, man. I'm saying she's a nice little solution to your problem."

Distracting thoughts of marriage and honeymoon nights, bare shoulders and a willing woman, *that* woman, drifted though Devin's mind. Devin and the diamond? The possibility intrigued him, and Devin had never turned his back on a challenge. Hadn't he started his business despite every possible obstacle? Wasn't he finally shaking loose the remnants of his childhood?

Devin shook his head to clear his thoughts. "What are you talking about, Jerry?"

"Just your gal-pal and that twenty-thou you owe a certain, um, loan manager."

Devin turned. "I don't owe it." A technicality, but true. After his dad's stroke, Devin had said he'd cover the debt. Too bad for him the creditor was more vile than the worst thug in a Scorsese gangster flick.

Jerry shrugged. "Your pop, you. Same difference. You stepped in, so now it's yours."

Devin moved closer to the pub, out of the way of the foot traffic on the sidewalk. "What scheme are you crafting?"

"You ever read any of Montgomery Alexander's books?"

Devin shook his head. "Never."

"Well, I have. Every one. They're all about this dude who's your average, everyday super-spy named Joshua Malloy. A real slick number. All the books are pretty much the same. Old Joshua's hired by some government to fight terrorists, assassinate the enemy, that kinda thing."

He popped a karate chop toward Devin. "Fire fights, supersonic jets, nuclear bombs. Sex. You name it, these books got it." Jerry grinned. "They ain't literature, but they're a damn wild ride."

Blond curls, petite features and delicate hands flashed through Devin's mind. "And that wisp of a woman writes these things?"

"Who'da thunk it, huh? For years people been wonderin'. 'Who is Montgomery Alexander?' they ask. Navy SEAL? Former CIA? Lot of folks say he's a retired spy carryin' a grudge. Got tired of his life being top secret and decided to call it fiction."

"So you're saying nobody knows what we just overheard?"

"You kiddin'?" Jerry lowered his voice. "This is major scoop material. I'll tell you something else. Nobody, I mean nobody, woulda guessed Alexander was the homecoming queen."

Devin looked down the bustling street, but her cab was well out of sight. His first impression had been right. She was one hell of a woman. And she'd taken a taxi right out of his life.

Idiot. He should have raced through the bar, fallen at her feet, shouted bad poetry over the loudspeaker. Something, *anything*, to have kept her close to him.

"Well," Jerry prodded. "What do you think?"

"About what?"

"Come on, Dev." He gripped Devin's shoulders and groaned with exaggerated melodrama. "The perfect scam just walked into our little corner of the world."

Devin jerked away. "I run a pub. That's not my world. And when I hired you, you promised me it wasn't yours anymore."

"I'm clean, man. I been straight over a year, ever since you hired me. But you need that money, and opportunity just strolled by. You can't tell me you didn't think of it. You're a chip off the old block, eh? And your pop was among the best."

"I'll get the money, Jerry," Devin insisted.

"What? In two weeks? How? This place is mortgaged to the hilt, buddy boy, and I know you don't got any spare cash tucked in a drawer somewhere. What're you gonna do? Call Derek?"

Devin grimaced. His older brother had been more than happy to follow in their father's footsteps. On the night Devin moved out, Derek had told him in no uncertain terms that he was a loser, would never make it in the legitimate business world, and would come crawling back with his tail between his legs. Every cruel word was a prophecy Devin had no intention of fulfilling.

"I'll get it. Without Derek and without pulling a con."

Jerry held up his hands in surrender. "See, this is what I been talkin' about." He gestured to Devin and then back to himself. "You and me, we ain't communicatin'. I'm not talkin' 'bout *conning* nobody. The thought never even entered my mind."

"Sure, Jerry."

"Honest. A simple business deal. You do something for diamond-lady, she does something for you."

Twenty grand weighed on Devin's shoulders. If Jerry really did have an idea, didn't he owe it to himself to listen? And if Jerry's idea wasn't legitimate, he could just walk away.

Fighting against his better judgment, Devin looked into Jerry's eyes. "You've got five minutes."

JERRY LET OUT a low whistle. "Man, you are gonna knock 'em dead. If this were a movie you'd be a shoo-in for an Oscar." He was sprawled in the middle of Devin's tattered but comfortable couch, the major piece of furniture in the tiny, rent-controlled apartment. Piles of paperback novels teetered on either side of him. Index cards and empty cans of soda littered the glass-topped coffee table, replacing Devin's financial magazines that were now scattered across the floor.

Devin chuckled. "Yeah, well, thanks for the vote of confidence. But I'm not interested in anything beyond the girl. She's where my head is tonight."

"The girl's money, you mean," Jerry said, slapping a sticky note inside one of the books.

"Of course," Devin lied. First rule of the con—always keep your eye on the ball—and he'd already blown it.

His head knew the money was the only reason he'd finally agreed to this little scam. Unfortunately, his heart and certain other parts of his body were preoccupied with the thought of seeing Paris again. Of getting close to her. Talking to her.

Touching her.

His head was planning a scam, and his heart was planning a seduction.

Wonderful. His first con in over ten years and he couldn't even focus. The woman had really thrown him for a loop.

But for the most part, he wasn't worried. Jerry's instinct was right. As a teenager, Devin had worked the streets enough with his dad to know he had a knack for playing whatever role needed to be played. Once he got the old rhythm back, Devin could practically sleepwalk through a con and pull it off.

That thought fostered another. Why not combine some not so pleasant business with some very pleasant pleasure? As long as when all was said and done he had twenty grand in his pocket, he might as well make the most of it. And other than paying off his dad's debt, about the only good thing that could come out of the whole mess was the chance to spend a little time with Paris.

He moved to the apartment's one bedroom and studied his reflection in the full-length mirror. He'd never really thought of himself as the suave, sophisticated baccarat type. More the jeans, T-shirt and poker type, actually. But he had to admit he looked the part. All it took was a close shave, some hair dye, and a double-dose of attitude and he was in like Flynn.

How easy it was to fall back into old habits. Bad habits.

His stomach churned and he pinched the bridge of his nose. *Dammit. What the hell was he thinking?*

He ripped off the suit jacket and threw it on his bed, then stormed out of the bedroom, determined to rectify this mistake before it went any further.

"Forget it, Jerry. I've changed my mind. I'm not conning her." No matter how much he needed the money, he wasn't going to scam Paris. He'd walked away from that life the day he turned eighteen. And not even the prospect of seeing her again could entice him back into that role.

Jerry closed a paperback crammed full of yellow sticky notes and stood up. "You'll be doin' her a favor, buddy boy. You heard the lady. She needs an Alexander."

He tossed the book to Devin. "And here you are, a walkin', talkin', breathin' solution to her little problem."

Devin studied the sketch on the back cover. The artist had been careful not to include anything too specific in the loose drawing. But even so, the resemblance was there. He could pass for Alexander. Easy.

"Your diamond gal's up a tree. You heard 'em. Don't you think she'd pay twenty grand to find the perfect Alexander?"

"She probably would," Devin agreed.

"Well, then," said Jerry, as if he'd just resolved some mathematical theorem.

"But she *didn't* hire me. I'm crashing the party, remember? That's how we know it's a con and not gainful employment."

"For cryin' out loud, Devie-boy. Where's the harm? I mean, we've already decided she'd pay it, right? And it sure ain't no worse than the con she's got going."

That lost Devin. "What con?"

Jerry spread open his arms. "Everything. The whole shebang. Letting the world think this Alexander dude exists. That he's smoking cigars and driving fast cars and sidling up to the ladies, when really he's a chick, fussin' over her hair, painting her toenails and taking bubble baths."

A pounding at the front door jerked Devin's mind away from images of Paris lounging in a tub full of bubbles.

"Expecting someone?"

Devin shook his head, frowning. His Manhattan apartment might not be in a high security building, but nobody was supposed to be able to enter without first being buzzed in. "Probably a neighbor." Still, he had a bad feeling...

He looked out the peephole. Nobody. The mailman had probably left Devin's mail in Mrs. Miller's box again. He'd given her his phone number three times, but the poor old thing just kept on risking a coronary by trotting up three flights of stairs and leaving his mail under the welcome mat.

When he opened the door, instead of his mail he found a small package, neatly wrapped in white paper and tied with string. A very bad sign.

Jerry looked over his shoulder. "They got your number, man."

With some trepidation, Devin picked up the package and dropped it on his kitchen table. Using a steak knife, he cut the twine and loosened the paper. A wave of nausea swept over him.

A cow's tongue. Fresh from any butcher shop in the city.

"It's a warning, my friend." Jerry's voice was lower and more serious than Devin had ever heard. "If you don't pay up on time, it'll be your tongue. Or your dad's."

Devin nodded, fighting back the urge to fly down the stairs and comb the streets for the punk who'd left that little gift. But that wouldn't help. It would only up the stakes.

Pop had always been small-time. Little cons. Just enough to pay rent and put food on the table. But his damn gambling habit had mushroomed. First the track, then Atlantic City.

His dad's biggest mistake had been placing a bet with Carmen's boys, then letting it ride, double or nothing, when the pony lost. Carmen and his cronies had sucked the old man in like quicksand. And mob-backed bookies weren't quick to forgive. Forget interest rates, it was the penalties that really got you.

"It's your choice, man. Either call Derek or..." Jerry's voice trailed off as he glanced toward the books on the sofa.

Trapped, Devin shut his eyes. Jerry was right. There was no way in hell he was going to call his brother. He'd run out of choices. He'd do this.

For his father, he would pull one last con.

PARIS TOOK A DEEP BREATH, then another. It didn't help. Panic inched another step closer.

The first hour of the party had been painless. She had circulated among the crowd, making small talk, evading questions about Alexander, and having a better time than she'd expected. But now people were beginning to wonder why Alexander hadn't arrived. And that meant it was almost curtain time.

She pressed her back against the wall, hoping no one would notice her and decide to chat. Right now, Paris wasn't sure she could form a coherent sentence. But despite her frazzled nerves, she had to concede the party was a hit. Cobalt Blue Publishing had rented the back two dining areas of a funky restaurant tucked away on the first floor of a renovated older hotel where Paris frequently stayed.

As she had wandered through the party earlier, she'd overheard various snippets of lively conversations. Everything from speculation about whether Alexander would really show, to intellectual ruminations about the deeper meaning behind some of Alexander's plots. A few people even asked if she was involved with Alexander *that way.* She'd said "no," of course, although for a fleeting moment she'd been tempted to reveal to the public the steamy affair she had going on in her fantasies. That was an urge she'd quelled right away.

But while Alexander might be the man of the hour, his absence wasn't keeping the guests from taking full advantage of the music, the food and the drink. A band Paris recalled seeing on late night television jammed in one corner under a wall of neon beer signs. A few energetic souls were dancing on a raised platform, but for the most part people clustered near the food or the alcohol. Two open bars bracketed a buffet laden with typical cocktail party appetizers. Nothing particularly original, but all tasty. Mounted behind the buffet, a six-foot-tall reproduction of the cover of Montgomery Alexander's latest book, *Dearest Enemy, Deadly Friend*, loomed over the crowd, a not-so-subtle reminder that this party had a purpose.

Paris had to hand it to Ellis Chapman. Once again he'd outdone himself. The owner of Cobalt Blue, Ellis had grown his small press into a legitimate publisher. Now he was on the brink of being a real industry player, primarily because of his guerilla marketing stunts. At a minimum, Ellis insisted his authors do local television talk shows, and it had originally irritated him when Paris explained that Alexander refused to make public appearances. Ellis being Ellis, he'd quickly turned the situation to his advantage by focusing on Alexander's mystique. If Paris were a betting woman, she'd lay odds that Ellis had planted the persistent rumors that Montgomery Alexander was a former spy.

She'd hoped Ellis would stay happy with the mysterious recluse angle indefinitely. But with the release of *Dearest Enemy*, he'd become antsy. Sales were doing just fine, but he wanted them to do even better. So when the book made one of the bestseller lists, he'd sent out invitations to a supposedly low-key cocktail party honoring the book's success. Then he'd hinted to the right people that Alexander himself might drop by.

When Paris had protested, he'd started throwing around words like "hardback," and "higher royalties," and "multi-book deals." At the same time, he'd casually asked Paris to let Alexander know he'd be seeing none of those things if he didn't get himself to New York for the cocktail party.

Now the restaurant overflowed with a variety of people who'd been drawn by the allure of seeing the reclusive Mr. Alexander. Reporters danced with editors. Fans chatted with other Cobalt Blue authors. A few soap opera stars mugged for the photographers.

Paris caught sight of Ellis chatting in the corner with a reporter she recognized from that morning's news. She swallowed the lump in her throat and wondered what he would do when she made her announcement that Alexander wasn't coming. Her gaze swept over the relatively well-mannered crowd. Surely this group wouldn't transform into a modern-day lynch mob.

Would it?

Swaying to the rhythm of the music, Rachel approached with two glasses of champagne and pushed one toward Paris.

"You know I don't drink that stuff."

"Trust me on this one."

Paris sniffed the champagne, sighed, then took a quick sip. The bubbles tickled her nose and took her mind off the party. Since that wasn't a bad thing, she took a bigger swallow.

"Having fun?"

"Better than I expected." She frowned, remembering

the announcement she still had to make. "For now, anyway." With a broad wave of her arm, Paris gestured over the entire room. "Look at this. Put these folks in pinstripes and it would be just like all the parties back when my dad was hot and heavy into politics. I spent the first twenty years of my life promising myself I would spend the rest of my life avoiding any function where I was required to schmooze. But here I am of my own free will."

"It's a fun party. And you're not the same girl who turned down Daddy's offer to run his law practice when he became a judge."

Paris nodded. That was true. She'd changed a lot since law school. If her dad had asked the woman she was now to follow in his footsteps, maybe she'd have been able to turn him down honestly, telling him she wanted to try her hand at writing. And if she was having a really brave day, she might even have told him what kind of writing—fast-paced, sexually charged, testosterone-laden flights of fancy.

Unfortunately, Judge Sommers hadn't asked today's Paris. He'd asked a Paris who existed almost a decade ago. Fresh out of law school, *that* Paris didn't have the stomach to stand up to her father. That Paris couldn't bear the look of disapproval she knew would have flashed across his face. So she'd concocted a job in another city and never told him about her books.

She grimaced. Who was she kidding? Today's Paris wasn't any braver. She'd managed to dig herself in deep with this life full of lies. But she'd get back on track soon enough. She had her literary and financial life all mapped out, and she didn't intend to keep secrets from her dad forever. As soon as she could afford to quit writing the Alexander books, she would. She'd turn to accepted literature. The kind that got reviewed in Sunday newspaper inserts. The kind that won literary awards.

The kind her dad would find respectable.

She tossed back the last of her drink, grabbed Rachel's still untouched one, and took a gulp.

Rachel's eyes widened. "Just because I'm the poster girl for step aerobics doesn't mean I can carry you back to your room."

"I think I've discovered the cure for nerves," said Paris, raising her glass. "Tiny bubbles." She hummed, trying to remember the words to one of her dad's favorite songs, her feet tapping out a subtle little jig.

"Paris."

"Hmm?"

"It's about time."

"They're going to hate me. What's that saying? Kill the messenger?"

"Nonsense. Maybe you won't get Christmas cards, but they won't hate you. They won't hate Alexander, either. It's just a delay, remember? Until we can find the right guy. In the meantime, this will just add to his mystique. Hell, it'll probably boost sales."

"Maybe I should—"

"Paris. Go."

Paris grimaced, but nodded. Walking like a woman condemned, she crossed the dance floor and headed toward the kitchen. On the way, she noticed a commotion near the entrance. Camera flashes illuminated the room like tiny bursts of lightning.

On any other day, Paris would have been lured by the possibility of seeing a big celebrity. But right now, even Harrison Ford couldn't have waylaid her. She had to get to the phone, pretend to dial, then return to the party and relay the sad news that Mr. Alexander had missed his flight from London.

A thunderous round of applause stopped her dead in her tracks. Curious, she turned and watched as the crowd parted to make way for a man she knew. A man who didn't exist.

Montgomery Alexander was walking straight toward her.

2

OF COURSE, Paris knew the man couldn't be Montgomery Alexander. Alexander was a figment of her imagination, created so she wouldn't have to explain why she was writing books filled with guns and cars and girls wearing next to nothing.

For years, she'd shared with him the kind of adventures she craved. Adventures a politician's daughter just couldn't have. In her mind, they'd traveled to exotic islands, danced until dawn, made love on the beach with nothing but the breeze to cover them. Real life couldn't satisfy her desire for passion and romance, but Alexander had filled that gap.

They'd had long conversations in the moonlight, and he'd listened to her hopes, her dreams. He amused her with his wit and beguiled her with his charm. Yes, she'd made him up. She knew that. But somehow she'd fallen in love with him anyway.

And over the years, she'd spent uncounted delightful hours imagining every luscious inch of him. So how was it possible that now Alexander's details escaped her? Now, she could see only *him*, an Alexander bursting free of fantasy and striding toward her with such purpose that her sluggish imagination kicked back into gear, conjuring up all sorts of erotic fantasies about how they could pass a little time together.

He stepped out of the shadows and she swallowed. *Oh my.*

His walk marked him as confident, almost arrogant, and his firm, humorless mouth was belied by a sparkle in his eyes that reflected compassion and intelligence. Defined cheekbones and a sturdy jaw accented his freshly shaved face. Dark brown waves were slicked back in a devil-may-care style.

Even the forest green suit, Alexander's standard attire for special occasions, was perfect. Another man might just wear the suit. Not Alexander. He commanded it, as if even clothing couldn't escape the brute force of his magnetism.

Alexander glanced her way, then said something to a nearby woman, who turned to the crowd with the promise that Mr. Alexander would be right back.

Before Paris realized what was happening, before she could still the flutter in her chest, he caught up with her. Her breath caught as his gaze caressed her, starting at her toes, and she surprised herself by trembling under the scrutiny. She took inventory of her appearance—black heels, little black dress with spaghetti straps, pinned-up hair—and wondered if he approved.

When he reached her face, Paris saw real desire in his eyes and fought hard not to blush. When he leaned in and kissed her cheek, she almost dissolved into a puddle of goo right there.

Her logical half knew she should be throwing a fit, hurling accusations and demanding explanations. Baser instincts urged her to grab the moment, to melt into his arms and taste his kisses. She concentrated on just keeping her balance.

"We shouldn't keep meeting like this," he said, his

voice straight from her fantasies. "People will say we're in love."

Paris gasped, knocked even more off-kilter. A right-punch to her stomach wouldn't have shocked her as much. He was quoting a line from her first book, and Paris wasn't sure if she should be comforted, or very, very worried.

She took a shaky breath. "Have you read the book?"

He hesitated. "Why do you ask?"

Paris shrugged. "No reason," she said, trying hard to throw some ice into her tone and take control of, not only the situation, but her own leaping pulse. "It just seemed like an odd line to choose, since Joshua, the hero, says it to a female spy after she's tried to kill him three times."

"I assume she fails."

Paris squirmed, aware that her own insides had turned to jelly with nothing more than the simple brush of his lips across her cheek.

"She doesn't kill him, right?" the stranger pressed.

"He, um, he manages to convince her otherwise."

"You mean he seduces her and manages to turn her into a counteragent. Nice technique he had, wouldn't you say?"

"Under the circumstances, I suppose," Paris muttered, trying to get a grip on herself.

Discussing a seduction scene with a man who could reduce her to quivers with one heated look was not a good idea. It was bad enough to have a crush on a man her imagination had conjured up, but that could be justified as a creative mind working overtime. But to have a libidinous reaction to some practical joker who was surely little more than a wanna-be actor was just plain ludicrous...no matter how much he looked and acted like the man of her dreams.

She needed to sit down, but nothing was nearby. Squatting on the floor would give entirely the wrong impression, and running screaming from the room simply wouldn't do. She had no choice but to stick it out.

"Who are you and why are you here?"

"Isn't it obvious?" The mild accent hinted at New York, not the cultured, almost British lilt she'd always imagined. Even so, it was familiar. She was just too rattled to remember why, who, where.

As if observing herself in a dream, she felt her features smooth into a polite mask punctuated by a sugary smile. "We need to talk."

"We're not talking?" His voice was almost a whisper. Sultry. Sexy.

For a moment, Paris thought that talking wasn't all it was cracked up to be. Kissing would be better. If she melted from nothing more than a peck on the cheek, imagine what a real, deep, mind-numbing kiss would do to her...

She gave herself a mental kick in the pants. He was *not* Alexander. He couldn't be. And she wasn't going to let herself crumble in a pile of lust at his feet.

"We need to talk now," she repeated. He nodded, just barely, and pressed his hand against her lower back, guiding her toward the kitchen. His heat through the thin material distracted her, and it took all her concentration to keep her feet moving and her lips smiling.

As they moved toward the kitchen, a few people called out to him, one or two holding out a hand for him to shake, and all urging him to stop and join the party. If he stepped away from her now and started circulating among the crowd, Paris knew she'd lose what little control over the situation she still had. She held her breath, waiting for him to play his trump card. He never did. Instead, he greeted the fans with a polite smile and a promise to return. With his hand firmly on her back, he steered them both through the mass of people and into the kitchen. Even Alexander couldn't have handled the situation any better.

She stepped away from him the second they were through the doors. She needed to get centered, to put on a businesslike front. Staying close to him would be too distracting. Too dangerous. Alexander or not, the man was lethal.

"Just who do you think you are?" she demanded.

No glib answer rolled past his lips. He offered no reassurance that all was well. Instead, his lips curved into the slightest of smiles. "Tonight, I'm Montgomery Alexander."

There it was, that punch in the stomach. For a moment, one freakish, funky, never-to-be-repeated moment, Paris believed him. The thought skittered through her head that all these years *she'd* been the one impersonating *him*.

Determination gripped her. He was trying to confuse her. Then she remembered where she had seen those eyes. The hair was no longer blond, and the roguish beard had been shaved, but there was no mistaking his midnight blue eyes.

"Alexander's eyes are darker," she said, her words and tone both an accusation and a challenge. "Almost black." Piercing, yet sensual. A contrast to this man's warm, inviting eyes—eyes that looked as though they could see all her secrets.

"Really?" He ran his finger casually down her arm, leaving her flesh hot and anxious in his wake. "Are you sure?"

She swallowed. She wasn't sure of anything. Except that the evening was becoming increasingly surreal and that she needed to regain her equilibrium before she lost complete control of the situation, and herself. It was as if a chasm yawned in front of her, compelling her to jump in, to free-fall into fantasy with this man. To live the adventure she'd always imagined.

Frowning, she urged her meandering thoughts back on track. "The other day. You're that waiter..." she said, latching on to the one small thing she was sure about.

"Actually, I own the bar."

"I don't care if you own the whole city. What are you doing here?" With a start, she realized how she'd been set up. "Rachel put you up to this."

"No."

"Don't give me that. How much is she paying you?" The words spilled over each other. "I'm going to kill her. I can't believe she would hire you without telling me."

She slammed her fist into the palm of her other hand. "Look at me. I'm a wreck. My best friend's made me a total wreck."

"Paris," he whispered.

She ignored him.

"Paris." He cupped her chin, easing her head up until she had to look at him. He dropped his hand and waited.

"What?"

"No one sent me," he said.

Maybe it was the gentle sound of his voice. Maybe it was something noble in his eyes. Paris wasn't sure. All she knew was that, despite circumstances and logic, she believed him.

And she wanted him to touch her again. She pushed the thought away, determined not to fall victim to the allure of this stranger. No matter how delicious the prospect.

"Then why are you here?" she demanded.

This time the confident curve of his lips became a full-fledged smile. It was everything she'd imagined Alexander's smile would be, and more. He reached out to caress her cheek, then pulled away as if he'd been caught in the cookie jar.

A wave of disappointment crashed over Paris as his hand retreated. She fought the urge to lean forward into his touch.

"It's nothing nefarious. I promise. I just wanted to meet you. To help you." He looked straight into her eyes. "Actually, I wanted to ask you out."

She blinked. "Oh. Well, you've got strange ideas about how to get a date." Her retort came out softer than she'd intended. She wasn't sure she believed him, but regardless, her indignation seemed to be sliding away. For a figment of her imagination, he'd become decidedly real. Not to mention sexy.

Stop it! This man was *not* Alexander. He was some anonymous party crasher who obviously had an agenda.

If the situation weren't so absurd, it would have been tragic. Here she was, faced with some weirdo—albeit a seductive, mind-numbingly gorgeous weirdo—impersonating her livelihood, and she was all a-flutter. Like some prepubescent groupie.

She realized he'd been observing her with some apprehension, the way a trainer would study a wild animal he intended to tame. "Is that all you have to say?" She heard the edge of impatience in her voice.

"What else can I say? The situation is in your hands. Are you going to turn me in?"

Paris was half-tempted to say yes, but both she and this stranger would know she was lying. She couldn't reveal him as a fraud without looking absurd herself, and certainly not without producing the "real" Montgomery Alexander. She had no choice but to continue the charade.

She needed him. And he damn well knew it.

Of course, there was a bright side. Ellis had made his rules very clear—no Alexander, no hardback or multi-book contract. Now, that little hurdle had been satisfied.

"Well?" he prodded. "What are you going to do?"

Through the window in the swinging kitchen door, Paris saw Brandon Foster, Montgomery Alexander's editor, approaching fast. That nailed her decision.

"Just remember who you're not, and don't do anything to get either of us in trouble." She smoothed her dress, trying to gear up for her impromptu performance. Then she pushed through the door, the evening's Alexander at her heels.

As soon as Brandon was close enough to overhear, Paris planted a kiss on both of the stranger's cheeks in stereotypical New York fashion, but still slow enough to absorb his scent. It reminded her more of a redwood forest than the streets of Manhattan. Primitive, earthy and masculine.

"Alexander," she scolded gently in a voice loud enough for Brandon, "I was beginning to think you'd missed your flight."

The last bit of wariness faded from the stranger's eyes, and the corner of his mouth twitched just slightly. Then he swung an arm around her and pulled her close, as if he'd held her that way a million times before. Automatically, she melted against him, her head resting against his shoulder.

"Sommers, I'm surprised. You know I'd never let you down."

This man had done his homework. Only one magazine article mentioned that Alexander called his manager by her last name of Sommers, just as she routinely referred to him only as Alexander.

"Good to finally meet you, old man," said Brandon, extending his hand. "I can't believe that for six years you didn't make an exception and let me meet you in person."

Paris watched as Brandon quit pumping Alexander's hand. *Had she just thought of him as Alexander again? Stop that. He's not Alexander. He's a stranger.* She pulled out of his embrace. His nearness must be making her confused.

"Not everything's entirely in my control." The stranger's voice was more clipped and less New York than it had been when they were alone. A remarkable performance, really. She had the feeling she was watching an actor playing a duke or some other British noble.

Then the stranger's last words registered, and Paris opened her mouth to protest. Was he suggesting she'd kept Alexander away from Brandon?

Brandon cocked his head toward Paris. "So our little angel here kept us apart, eh?"

"I'm afraid so."

How dare he! "I never—"

"She's kept me locked in a basement in London, a sex slave chained to a typewriter, for the past few years."

Her jaw dropped, even as wicked and surprisingly appealing images flashed through her head.

Brandon's eyes went wide. "You two are a—"

"No," Paris interjected. "No, we're not."

"I was just pulling your chain, old man. I leave the business end to Sommers because I don't have the stomach for the grinder you literary types put my manuscripts through." Alexander's smile broadened. "Without Sommers I'd probably go into a less stressful career. Like espionage."

Paris could have kissed him. Not only had he confirmed her story that it was the author, not the manager, who was the recluse, but he'd hinted at a background in espionage.

Whether Ellis had started it or not, the long-standing rumor that the books were fictionalized accounts of Alexander's life as a spy seemed to boost sales, so she certainly wasn't going to complain. Besides, in her mind, the line between Alexander and his hero had always been a bit murky. Except for the fact that he didn't actually exist at all, the author Alexander was every bit as much the poised, polished secret agent as the fictional hero, Joshua Malloy.

She looked at the stranger, who was chatting amiably with Brandon. With his drop-dead good looks, tailored suit and unflappable air, he seemed to have Alexander down pat. Hell, he claimed he *was* Alexander, at least for tonight. *Absurd.*

But the champagne, the party, her stranger—they were a heady mix. She wouldn't admit it out loud, didn't even want to admit it to herself, but for tonight she wished it could be true. She wished he really were Alexander.

When he looked her way, she smiled, then concentrated on the floor. Maybe it was just the champagne, but part of her was starting to believe he really was.

Paris shook her head to banish such ridiculous thoughts. No matter how much her body sizzled when he touched her, no matter how many goose bumps she got when she looked at him, she had no business thinking *that way* about her mystery man.

Why not? She bit her lip. Why not, indeed? Wasn't this man exactly what she'd always wanted? A slice of fantasy wrapped up in a tailored suit? A finite package of adventure chock-full of enough charisma to nourish her for the rest of her life? Didn't she want an adventure to sustain her? And hadn't Mr. Adventure arrived before her on a silver platter?

Her rational side objected before she got carried away, listing all the reasons why she had no business getting involved with him. Not as much fun, perhaps, but certainly more reasonable, more rational.

Brandon interrupted her debate by running down a list of people Alexander needed to meet during the evening. "Especially Ellis Chapman. This party was his idea, you know."

"Well, then, he certainly should be on the list," Alexander agreed.

"I suppose I should go and find him," added Brandon. "After all, normally we'd already be well acquainted and have no need for this introductory period."

Paris wondered if Alexander had caught the criticism in Brandon's voice.

Alexander nodded slowly, as if digesting Brandon's suggestion. "If we'd known each other, it would have been a different Montgomery Alexander. I'm only me, and I make no apologies for my quirks. But if you want me to say I would have enjoyed drinking a beer with you on my deck, and it's a shame circumstances prevented it, then I will. And Brandon," Alexander added, "I'll mean it, too."

Brandon's expression softened. "Every interview has said you are both an enigma and a gentleman. Every interview has been right." Brandon shook Alexander's hand again, nodded at Paris and then disappeared into the center of the room.

Paris realized she was holding her breath.

Alexander took her hand and tugged her toward the middle of the room. "Don't you think it's time we mingle?"

"I'm not sure we should."

"Afraid I'm going to blow your cover?" He dragged his fingertips in lazy strokes up and down her palm, each pass sending her blood throbbing.

"I...I was."

"And now?"

She eased her hand free, not sure she was comfortable with the way her entire body seemed to sigh with each caress. "Right now you're batting a thousand. I'm wondering if you can keep it up."

"Sommers, I'm shocked." He held up his hands and pulled a face of mock disbelief. "Here I've been slaving for at least eight hours to read up on good ol' Mr. Alexander and his very pretty manager, and you're questioning my ability to cram. I crammed before every test in high school. I've got it down to an art form."

Paris restrained herself from laughing. "Yes, but did you pass those exams?"

He waggled a finger. "No fair asking hard questions."

"That does it. We're staying in this corner. If they really want to talk, they can come to you." Besides, she wanted to figure out his angle.

"Of course." He moved closer, but didn't touch her. He didn't have to. His proximity alone made her head spin.

"What's that supposed to mean?"

"Just that you must be pretty attracted to me if you're going to that much trouble to keep me all to yourself."

She smiled sweetly, fighting to keep her breathing under control. "Haven't you ever heard the saying? Keep your friends close, but your enemies closer?"

"So we're enemies?"

"Frankly, I have no idea."

"Well, there you go." He leaned against the wall, smug satisfaction dancing across his face.

"There I go what?"

"Just that you don't know if I'm an enemy or a friend. But you want me around. Sounds like attraction."

She held her tongue. Such an infuriating man. *Attraction* wasn't the point. The point was that he crashed the party—pretending to be the man of the hour—supposedly to get a date. Then, in a display of pure arrogance, assumed she was attracted to him. The idea was irritating, conceited. It was also, she conceded, exactly what Alexander would assume.

Well, so what? True, he looked the part. And he did have a certain aura. And, yes, there was a tingle when he took her hand. But that didn't mean...

Okay, maybe it did. But even if Paris was attracted to him, he would be the last person she'd tell. "I think you're confusing curiosity about your lack of manners and good character for attraction," she finally retorted.

"Am I?"

His response was so quick that for a moment words evaded her, and he seized the advantage.

"Let me prove myself. Let me be your knight in shining armor and ride forth into the masses spreading the glorious crusade of Montgomery Alexander." He thrust one arm skyward as if holding a sword.

A giggle escaped her. She couldn't help it. He looked so silly. Besides, what choice did she really have? Montgomery Alexander hiding in the corner with his manager would do nothing to satisfy his fans and would certainly not make Ellis Chapman's day. Any minute now, the masses would come to them.

It's just like swimming. Take a deep breath and jump.

"Fine," she said. "But we go together."

Arms linked, they plunged forward. Within moments, someone caught Alexander's attention and pulled him toward the dance floor, but not before he leaned over and offered one last word of reassurance.

"Don't worry," he said. "I promise an award-winning performance."

"I SHOULD HAVE COME right over," Rachel said. "But I thought you'd hired him, and I was going to sulk a little since you'd kept me out of the loop."

The party was winding down, and Rachel and Paris were camped out in the darkest corner of the restaurant. The remains of crackers, cheese and plump strawberries littered their table. Paris grabbed the last strawberry and shoved the plate aside.

"He's amazing," Paris said, glancing toward the dance floor where her mystery man was politely stalling a persistent redhead who kept urging him to dance. "I mean, his *performance* was amazing," she added, feeling the heat pool in her cheeks. "I shadowed him for two hours, ready to rescue him, but he never said anything stupid."

"Is he how you pictured Alexander?"

Paris shrugged. Rachel had hit upon the question of the hour. "It's weird. Before, I could imagine Alexander's hands, his scent, his walk, everything. But now, when I close my eyes, all I see is, well, him." She nodded toward the impersonator.

"Well, of course," Rachel purred, looking like the cat that swallowed the canary.

"Of course? Oh please, Dr. Freud, do enlighten me."

"Fantasy and reality collided. Reality is winning."

"You really do sound like Freud."

"I'm serious. You're attracted to him, and—"

"Whoa, wait a minute. I am not attracted to him."

"You're such a liar. Besides, where's the harm?"

"Just because he's attractive doesn't mean I'm attracted

to him." Paris wanted Rachel to see the difference. And she needed to convince herself there *was* a difference. Then Rachel's words registered. "Harm?"

"In a little seduction," explained Rachel. "Where's the harm in that?"

"He's not going to seduce me." *Too bad*, thought Paris, taking in his broad shoulders and leading man looks. She could think of worse things than being swept away by a man like that.

"No, no," continued Rachel. "*You* should seduce *him*."

"Oh, well that's...have you lost your mind?" Paris blustered, pulling her gaze away from Alexander.

"Don't tell me you haven't thought about it. He practically dropped out of the sky into your lap. He admits he wants to go out with you. What better way to get a boy toy?"

"Rachel!" She'd played with the idea earlier, true. Who wouldn't have? But there was no way she'd go through with it. Really. Rachel was just being ridiculous. For one thing, Paris wasn't the seducing type. And even if she was...

Well, she wasn't. So it didn't matter.

Paris felt Rachel's stare, then saw the diabolical grin.

"Uh-huh," said Rachel. "You know you want to. He's your fantasy come true." She grabbed her purse and hauled it onto her lap.

"I'm not looking for a fantasy," Paris urged, as much to herself as her friend. "You know my plan."

"Oh, right. Two more of these books. Sock away the money. Finish your dreary epic. Publish it under your real name. Retire Alexander. Admit to your father you're a writer, but of fine literature that won't embarrass the family name. Find a suitable man—that means boring, by the way—and have babies. The end. How could I have forgotten your brilliant plan?"

"You're going to use a lifetime's supply of sarcasm in one sitting. And there's nothing wrong with my plan," Paris insisted, ignoring the niggling feeling that maybe there was.

"Are you supposed to be a nun in the meantime?"

Paris squirmed, not wanting to admit just how appealing Rachel's seduction plan sounded. Instead, she parried, figuring that the best defense was a good offense. "You're not exactly practicing what you preach," she said, then immediately regretted her words.

Rachel shot her a tentative glance. "What's that supposed to mean?"

Paris shrugged, not sure it was the time or the place to explore the truckload of issues surrounding Rachel's love life. To say Rachel had self-confidence issues was an understatement. An overweight, plain little girl from the wrong side of the tracks, Rachel had been teased mercilessly during grammar school. And the torment had escalated in high school after Paris had moved away. She might have grown up and slimmed down and turned into a knockout, but Paris didn't think Rachel saw her true self in the mirror. And so she overcompensated something fierce.

"All I mean is that you've dumped the last dozen guys you've dated without so much as a good-night kiss. You're hardly the roving expert on seduction," Paris said. During their years together in college and law school, Paris had watched Rachel master the art of flirting. Now, she attracted a constant stream of men, but always cut them loose before they got too close. Paris didn't need a textbook on pop psychology to see why. Rachel couldn't handle being the one to get dumped, so she cut the possibility off at the pass. And as a result, she never got close to anyone.

"That's completely different," Rachel insisted. "The men I date are potential relationship material. When it's obvious things won't work out, I let them down gently." Paris opened her mouth to argue, but her friend didn't let her get a word in. "Besides, I'm not suggesting you marry this guy. You just need to have a little fun. Especially if the rest of your life is going to be the utter doldrums." Rachel continued to rummage in her purse, finally pulling out three little plastic packets. Condoms.

"For crying out loud, Rachel," Paris snapped, looking around to see if anyone had noticed. "I don't need these."

"Just take them," coaxed Rachel, opening Paris's purse and dropping them in.

Paris grimaced. The last thing she needed was to get involved with a guy who impersonated authors to get a date. *Even one so intriguing and sexy?* She shoved the thought away. She needed to focus on work...not long, steamy nights with Alexander or the waiter or whoever the hell he was.

Still, a little more time together would give her a chance to figure out what he was up to. And why not have a one-night fling? How many women had the chance to cuddle up to their fantasy man? She shivered from the memory of his taut, tight muscles. Of the way her body had caught fire from just the touch of his fingertip.

She sighed.

Get a grip, Paris.

No way was she going to bed with the guy. It simply was not going to happen. He wasn't Alexander, and that was the end of that. Plain and simple.

Except...

Already she missed the way her blood burned when he

looked toward her, missed the way her skin tingled when he was nearby. She grazed her teeth across her lower lip. She did want an adventure. And a tall, dark and handsome one had just materialized out of thin air. So maybe Rachel was right. Maybe a little seduction was in order.

No, no, no. She curled her hands into tight fists. Sleeping with him was out of the question. It would be a mistake—indulgent and foolish.

But why couldn't she spend a little more time with him? A little flirting would be innocent enough. What would be the harm in that?

Before her mind could think up a reason, she pushed herself out of her chair. "The party's wrapping up. I should go collect my Alexander."

3

BY THE END OF THE PARTY, Devin held new respect for actors. He'd been "on" for five hours. Three hundred minutes of smiling and hand-shaking. Eighteen thousand seconds of an award-winning performance.

He'd forgotten how much work it was to stay in character for so long. His head throbbed, fire lapped at his feet and demons tormented each muscle. If Paris knew how grueling the evening had been, she would gladly write his check.

Paris.

His body wasn't too tired to express extreme appreciation for the way the flimsy black dress hugged her, defying gravity with the help of two thin straps. He watched, enraptured, as she maneuvered through the last few guests, kissing cheeks and shaking hands. Primped and manicured, blond and bouncy, she was the complete opposite of the listless, life-weary women who had littered the streets of his childhood neighborhood.

She hypnotized him. Paris was everything Devin had ever hoped to find in a woman, but knew he could never have.

You don't belong here. Memories flooded back. His father, stressing diction and poise. His uncle, teaching him French. It never hurt for a grifter to have a touch of class, they'd said.

His schooling had started with street sessions. He and

his father pulling the old switcheroo and conning store owners out of change for a twenty, when he'd paid with only a fiver. The movie *Paper Moon* had shown that maneuver to the world, but still they'd never been caught. Easy cons, kid stuff. Then came the bigger deals. Scams that would prepare him for life on the street.

He knew his father had only been looking out for him, and Devin loved him for it. But he didn't love his father's life-style. So he'd spent a lifetime working and studying, all so he could escape his father's shadow, and this is where he'd ended up. Pulling a con on the most adorable woman he'd ever met.

"Hey stranger." She eased up beside him, linking her arm through his as if they'd stood together a hundred times. Her touch excited Devin as much as her familiarity saddened him. He fought the urge to pull her tight against him and cursed sentimentality. She was a mark. Nothing more. *Quit thinking you're better than your background.*

"Hey yourself," he said, shaking off the mood and matching her smile. "You left me. I was beginning to think you'd decided you could trust me alone."

Her grin blossomed, punctuated by a wink. "Not a chance. I've been keeping tabs on you from a distance."

"Have you? That's interesting." He'd injected a lascivious note into his voice. From the way she cocked her head, he was pretty sure she'd caught the inflection.

"Interesting? Why?" She pulled out the hairpins holding up her mass of blond curls. They tumbled down, and her fingers intertwined in one long strand. God, she was adorable.

"I've been keeping some tabs on you, too. I wonder if we've been thinking about the same thing."

Twirl, twirl. Devin didn't think Paris realized what she

was doing. A nervous habit, perhaps. But what was making her nervous? A little innocent flirting?

He raked his eyes over that dress again, taking in the way it clung to her delicious curves, then back up to her soulful eyes and sun-kissed hair. The beginning of an erection strained against his fly.

To hell with innocent. The woman was a siren.

"You said you came because you wanted to go out with me." Her voice held only the slightest tremor. "I was wondering if you meant that."

"Of course." Go out with her, hold her, touch her, taste the sweetness of her skin. Make love to her.

"The party's wrapping up. Are you tired?" The finger returned to that one strand of hair, and Devin imagined the soft lock caressing his chest, her fingers combing through his own hair as she lost herself to passion.

He'd lost his train of thought. "What?"

She hesitated. "Never mind. It was nothing. I'll just say good-night."

"No, no." He took her bare arm, delighting in its softness and anxious to know if the rest of her was as silky. Unable to help himself, he traced his finger up her arm, then across her delicate shoulder, and finally along the neckline of her dress. "Have a drink with me."

She took a shuddering breath. "I...I really shouldn't. It's late."

"*Then stay with me until it's early, and I'll ask you again.*"

She looked up, stern, but the desire in her dark eyes told a different story. "Have you memorized every one of my books?"

"Not at all."

"Just a few choice lines to help you get what you want?"

"Perhaps. Or maybe it's just coincidence."

"Coincidence?"

Devin kissed the back of her hand, letting his lips linger on the delicate skin. He wanted to taste more of her. All of her. "Maybe I'm coming up with these lines entirely on my own. I could be the man you've always dreamed of. Do you really want to risk turning me away?"

He expected her to laugh and say he wasn't the stuff of anyone's dreams, much less hers. It would break the ice, and they could have a relaxing drink, talk, and explore where this chemistry between them would lead. Her hotel room, perhaps? Heat coursed through him and he wondered if she'd be keen on skipping the drink, the talk.

But she wasn't laughing. Instead, her brow furrowed. Rather than putting him down, she took a step backward.

Okay, mistake in judgment. If he didn't regroup quickly, Devin would never get close to her. He frowned, remembering why he was really there.

He *had* to get close to her, had to bring up the money.

"Or not," he said, wishing he could think of something a little more articulate.

She squinted at him. "What?" Although only a few steps from him, it seemed as if she had retreated to the far side of the restaurant.

"I mean I did memorize your books. Well, not every book. A friend culled key lines. We put them on cue cards. I crammed."

A bug. That's what he felt like under her stare. A big, fuzzy bug pinned to acid-free paper and baking under a bare lightbulb.

"Cue cards?" she repeated.

Devin fished in his jacket pocket, finally pulling out a handful of note cards. He held one out like a peace offering.

She took it gingerly, as if it might bite.

"'My job? It's wild and dangerous, but not as dangerous as my passion for you.' Were you planning on using *that* line tonight?"

If Jerry were around, Devin might just have to kill him for including that card among the bunch. Since Jerry was safe and sound in Brooklyn, Devin chose another tact.

"Maybe. I like to keep my options open."

Her mouth twitched. "You do? Why?"

"Because I like to get what I want. And I'm willing to work for it."

Her eyes softened. "What do you want?"

"A lot of things." *Her.* To see raw, sexual heat reflected in her eyes. To know that right then, right there, she wanted him as much as he wanted her.

"For example, I've been wanting to do this all night." He heard her breath catch as he moved toward her. Eyes closed, she leaned toward him, soft and sweet and sexy. Desire radiated from her, and he knew she wanted his kiss.

Wanted *him.* Devin O'Malley, Montgomery Alexander, it didn't matter. She wanted the man standing next to her. No matter what name she might give him, tonight Devin was that man.

Molten desire boiled in his veins. His body craved the feel of her mouth under his, her fingers gliding over his skin, her breasts pressed hard against his naked chest.

Devin groaned, quelling the urge to take her mouth, to explore with his hands the secrets she had hiding under that sexy little dress. He wanted to let her excitement build slowly, even if it killed him. To wait until her head was just as sure as her body of how much she needed him close to her. Inside her.

His palms cupped her cheeks, pulling her closer. She trembled as his fingers glided across her skin, skimming over the top of her ears, then tangling deep in her loose curls.

She tilted her head back, her lips parted, eager and moist. Waiting. Waiting for him.

"Fabulous," he murmured.

"Yes," she whispered. "Fabul—"

She opened her eyes, still lazy and soft with desire. "Fabulous?" she asked. "My hair? That's what you've been wanting to do all night? Play with my hair?"

"It's hypnotic. Hair like that could have felled an entire army. Helen of Troy and all that." His voice was husky with lust, and it took every ounce of his strength to keep from touching his mouth to hers, to keep from giving her what she wanted. What he wanted, too.

"I'm...well, thank you, but..."

She frowned, and he knew she was trying to figure out his angle. "You really just wanted to touch my hair?"

The disappointment in her voice humbled him.

"Actually, there was something else."

She smiled, almost shyly, and his heart raced. "Yes?"

"I'd still like to buy you a drink."

She hesitated, her small tongue flicking over her lips. He held his breath. Was she, like him, wondering if maybe skipping a drink and going straight to her room might be the better plan? Or maybe she was trying to talk herself out of even the drink?

"All right," Paris agreed at last. "But just one drink."

He exhaled, relieved, and held his hand out to her.

"You have my word," he assured.

But after the drink...? Well, he'd make no promises about that.

HE KEPT HIS WORD, too, Paris thought. An hour later she was still sitting across from him in a secluded booth near the back of the hotel's deserted bar, one unfinished drink between them. Meant to serve twelve, the drink, called a "House on Fire," combined vodka, rum, banana liqueur, coconut and other fruit flavors into a concoction the menu said was a favorite at parties. Mystery Man and Paris hadn't made a dent.

He also hadn't made a pass. And despite the heated way he kept looking at her, she was starting to think that all he really wanted was the drink and a little small talk.

Well, what did you expect? He's your fantasy, but that doesn't mean you're his.

Paris sighed. She was beginning to feel like a tennis match was going on in her head. Yes, she wanted to sleep with Alexander. No, she didn't want to sleep with Mystery Man. Yes, no, yes, no.

The "no's," of course, were a lie. She *did* want to sleep with one of him, more than she'd ever wanted any man. But that would be a mistake. She needed to keep reminding herself. He wasn't Alexander, and sleeping with him would be a huge, giant, mind-blowing mistake.

Too bad. He'd barely even touched her and already her body mourned his absence.

"Something wrong?" he asked.

You're not touching me. That's what's wrong. But she didn't say it. Instead, she shook her head. "No, not at all."

Whatever game he was playing, she'd hold her own. She plucked a slice of orange out of the huge bowl that housed their mammoth drink. "I want to know about you. I mean, how on earth did you manage to end up here tonight?"

Alexander reached across the table to stroke her cheek, the caress electric and inviting. Without thinking, she pressed her face into his palm, soaking up the warmth before he pulled away. He didn't let the contact between them break, however. As soon as one hand left her face, the other took her fingers.

"You already know everything. Didn't you invent me?"

"I'm beginning to think I did." Paris's thoughts became fuzzy as she lost herself in his caress. Fingers intertwined as he traced the outline of her hand. His skin, slightly calloused, melded with hers that was lotioned and pampered. He dragged his fingernails lightly across her palm. The effect was torture, almost a tickle, and completely erotic in its casualness.

She blinked, then remembered to breathe. "Maybe I conjured you up in my head and you just fell from the sky like manna."

"So why did you make me up?"

Why indeed? How could she explain? She'd needed an author for her books, true. But that wasn't the whole story. She'd been lonely, plain and simple. And the sunsets in Texas, orange and purple and vibrant, were too perfect to share with just anyone. How many times had she sat, alone, above the river sipping coffee and waiting for the sun to set? She'd never met a man worthy of sharing her sunsets.

So she'd made him up.

She opened her mouth, trying to find the words to explain about twilight, then shut it again. That wasn't a secret she wanted to share.

"Paris?"

She took another sip while she collected her wits and considered what part of the truth to tell him. "Necessity."

"You had no choice but to write novels under a fake name?"

Paris laughed. "Are we talking about me, or philosophizing about free will?" She shrugged. "I thought it was necessary. It's even more necessary now."

"Why?" He leaned toward her, elbows on the table, his chin resting on his fists while still clasping her hand. As he slowly rubbed his chin along their joined hands, the slight prickle of his evening beard grazed her fingertips and his breath mingled with her skin. His earthy scent teased her, sending her head swirling to dizzying heights.

His appearance was innocent, like a fascinated student caught up in the wonder of learning. The effect was anything but innocent. Paris couldn't escape her body's reaction. Her palms were damp, her stomach fluttery. She wondered if he could see her tight nipples under the thin black dress.

Only their hands were touching. She wanted so much more.

"What's so special about Alexander?"

She gaped at him, letting his words sink in. Something clicked in her head. Montgomery Alexander didn't exist. So who was this man sitting across from her and making her pulse burn? Slowly she took her hand back. "What's with the twenty questions?"

"Maybe I want to get to know you."

"Or maybe you're up to something," she retorted, careful to lace her voice with a slight tease. She might want the truth, but she didn't want to scare him away getting it. She knew he wasn't Alexander. But he was close. And real. And sexy.

Just being there with him was more adventure than she'd ever had. And touching him, feeling the way she did when he touched her back, well, she could store that memory away and live on it forever.

Mystery Man leaned back in the booth, his eyes widening. "Up to something? Why on earth would you think that?'' She quirked an eyebrow, and was rewarded with his chuckle. "Fair enough. I'll grant that you've got a few good reasons.''

He took her hand, and she glanced down at their casually intertwined fingers. The touch lacked the earlier erotic caress, but the contact affected her all the same. She took a shaky breath and looked back up into his eyes.

"Really, Paris,'' he continued, the sparkle in his eyes matching the smile on his mouth. "I'd like to know. Why was I necessary?''

I? He spoke as if he really was Montgomery Alexander. Paris couldn't shake the feeling that she was having a drink with a man she had known for years, not just hours. A man she'd dreamed about forever.

Of course he wasn't Alexander, and for a second she thought she should argue with him, pursue uncovering whatever he was up to, at least for the sake of appearances. But the desire to share her secret with this enigmatic, fascinating man overwhelmed her. And that confused her even more than the fire that consumed her every time he looked her way.

"There were lots of reasons,'' she said, pulling her hand away and focusing on her words. She started to tick them off on her fingers. "I've always wanted to be a writer, but my dad never took my writing seriously. I love him to death, but it's no secret that a lot rides on the family name. He's a federal judge in Houston, the fifth in a long line of judges, with various other relatives owning companies, performing heart surgery, politicking.''

Paris heard his slight cough as she switched hands to offer more reasons. This talking was good. It proved his proximity hadn't killed her ability to form a coherent sentence.

"Does your mom know?''

"She died when I was three. I think that fueled Daddy's zest for watching out for his little girl. And mine for not wanting to disappoint him." She shrugged. "That's why I went to law school—Daddy wanted me to. But I came here for school, to New York I mean, and I wrote whenever I wasn't studying. About the time I graduated, I sold a story to *Desperado*, the men's magazine."

"Let me guess. You published under a pseudonym, figuring your dad wouldn't find out. *Desperado* also publishes pulp paperbacks, and they wanted one from you. And then another, and it snowballed."

"You're good. If you're wondering, the story ends with the good daughter telling Daddy that she's opening her own law firm. She moves back to Texas, but settles in Austin. She figured that was near enough to Houston to keep Daddy happy, but far enough for a little distance. And, surprise, surprise, she soon lands a major client, up-and-coming author Montgomery Alexander. Eventually, she becomes his manager. Daddy's proud, because she's doing well, but he's a little bit miffed that she spends so much time promoting the author of 'those kinds' of books."

Paris took a long sip of the drink before continuing. "So I've got myself stuck. I don't *want* to tell him because of his reaction to the books themselves, and I *can't* tell him now because it's ballooned so much."

"Does it bother you?"

Paris studied the pattern in her cocktail napkin, only half noticing that it required significant effort to see only one, not four, designs. "Daddy not knowing?"

"*Nobody* knowing."

"Some people know," Paris replied, feeling like a schoolgirl trying to argue her way out of a failing grade in a subject she'd never studied.

"Who?"

"Well, Rachel. And now you."

"Oh, yeah, lots of people know."

She heard the sarcasm.

"I didn't say lots. I said some people. You're 'some people.'" Two, actually. Montgomery Alexander and Mystery Man.

His dimple appeared. "Thanks for the vote of confidence."

She smiled at him, then sighed. "It doesn't matter anyway, because I won't be writing these books forever. I'm working on an epic novel. Very literary. Very Oprah."

"Does Brandon know?"

"That I'm writing a literary novel?"

"That you write these books that Daddy doesn't approve of."

"Isn't it my turn for questions?" Paris asked, wishing she were bold enough to suggest they just skip to the kissing part.

Thankfully, kissing wasn't sex, at least as long as they didn't get carried away. Which meant kissing was within the random boundaries she'd drawn within her plan, a loophole she'd quite happily exploit.

"Humor me."

Paris knew the big picture eluded her, but the alcohol was making her thoughts mushy. *Why was he asking these questions? What didn't he want her to know?* Before she could figure out how to challenge him, Alexander jumped in with another query.

"So why doesn't Brandon know? He seems like a nice guy."

"He is a nice guy. Same reason, I guess. I didn't think I could tell him at first, and now it's too late. Besides, I kind of like getting his unfiltered reaction to my work."

Kissing, she thought, trying to throw psychic energy his way. Forget Brandon and concentrate on kissing. She focused on his forehead and tried out Rachel's most seductive smile.

"Why didn't you just tell him at the beginning?"

So much for her psychic abilities. "If you knew Brandon, you'd understand. He started his career at *Desperado*. The most prominent thing in his office was a poster of six women wearing bikinis made out of the flag and toting rifles. It was on the wall next to his safari trophies."

She watched his face to make sure he had the scene firmly in mind. "Now picture me. Early-twenties, size six, frequently described by my friends as perky. I was afraid if he knew I wrote it, he'd ooze so much testosterone that the book would lose what little literary merit I'd managed to cram into the hundred and fifty thousand words."

"How'd you keep it a secret? What about royalty checks?"

She twirled her straw around the edge of the glass. That had been the tricky part. "Well, you could say my dad helped with that." His brow furrowed. "Law school, I mean. Just one afternoon of paperwork, and suddenly the Montgomery L. Alexander Literary Corporation was born. The company actually owns the copyrights to all of the books. And it has a tax identification number, so there's no problem with the IRS."

Alexander leaned back, nodding approval. "Very clever."

"Thanks." *Now can we move on to other topics? Perhaps, say, kissing?*

"But Brandon never asked?"

Paris took a long swallow of the drink. Obviously he was stuck in the getting-to-know-you phase while she was itching to start rounding bases. "Sure he did. I told him about Alexander being the private type, and that was that. Eventually he quit asking."

"You must have liked him, though. You're at another publisher, and he's still your editor."

"Same publisher, actually. Cobalt Blue's a recent spin-off of *Desperado*. Ellis Chapman thought the classy name would help with marketing," said Paris. "But you're right. Brandon's swell. He's a fabulous editor. And we've become good friends, too." She felt a blush creep to her cheeks. "At least, as much as we can be considering I lie to him pretty much every day."

Paris fell back against the plush upholstery, intending to nip in the bud his fascination with the fine art of conversation. "Listen to me babble. This drink on top of champagne. Wow." She drew the straw up to her mouth and licked off every drop of liquid, enjoying the reaction she saw in his eyes.

She didn't really doubt he wanted her. Throughout the entire evening, his touch, his look, his voice had all told her so. He wanted her and she wanted him.

But she wasn't going to have him. She was going to hold tight to her resolve. It was just chemistry between them, anyway. Nothing magic, nothing earth-shattering. She would allow herself a kiss, maybe even two or three, just so she'd have the memory. So she could satisfy the part of her that longed to be swept up and away, the part that wanted to lose herself if only for a moment.

She'd lose herself in his kisses. Those kisses, she told herself—*his kisses*—would be enough.

Of course, even a kiss might be wishful thinking. Like her or not, he still hadn't tried anything. *So what are you going to do about it?*

No brilliant plan stepped forward, and for the first time in her life Paris wished she'd paid more attention to Rachel's scripted, rehearsed and tested technique. She'd just have to wing it. Or chicken out entirely.

"Are you going to tell Brandon?" he asked.

She smiled at him, still teasing the end of the straw between her lips in a manner she hoped emphasized how kissable she was. "You'll be out of a gig if I do."

HER RESPONSE WAS LIGHT and teasing. But even so, Devin worried she had realized what his questions were getting at. If a number of people already knew Alexander's deep, dark secret, she'd have little motivation to pay him to keep his mouth shut.

His father's voice lectured in his head. *So what if she's figured it out? She'll realize when you ask her for the cash.*

True enough. But he didn't want to demand the money just yet. He wanted to get to know her, to spend time with her. Alone. Preferably undressed. From the way she looked at him, he knew she wanted to spend that type of quality time with him, too.

If he could just keep the desire burning in her eyes, maybe he could get the money and still manage to hold on to the girl.

He bit back a curse. Who was he fooling? She wasn't interested in him. Paris wanted Montgomery Alexander. She wanted to be swept away by a suave, sophisticated man who said all the right things.

Devin O'Malley was not that man. But he wanted her, wanted her bad. Even if it meant playing a part. And maybe, just maybe, she'd fall a little bit for the man behind the mask.

Oh, Devie-boy. Falling for a mark. Didn't I teach you better?

"Shut up," he whispered.

"What?" She looked confused. He hoped she hadn't heard him.

"I said we should go up."

She cocked an eyebrow. *"We* should?"

"I meant that I should walk you to your room."

"Oh." She studied her short manicured nails. Was she disappointed he hadn't suggested more?

"And then you'll invite me in for a nightcap." There. That was a very Montgomery Alexander thing to say.

"Pretty confident, aren't you?" she asked, her breathless voice reassuring him that he didn't have to worry about being invited in for the evening.

"That we'll have a nightcap together? Yes."

"Why, Mr. Alexander, are you trying to get me drunk?"

"I think you already are."

She put up a good show of being offended. *"Moi?* No, no, no. I'm just a little tipsy." She leaned forward, crooking her finger to draw him nearer. "If I were drunk, then I'd do what I've been thinking about all evening."

Devin's heart skipped a beat. "Yeah? What's that?"

A mischievous smile lit up her eyes, and he wondered what he was in for. In a quick movement, Paris slid out of the booth, and joined him on his side of the table. She sat close, her hip and thigh soft and feminine against him. Devin steeled himself against an instinctive, physical reaction. She was so close, so sweet. He wanted her so naked, so willing.

"What have you been wanting to do?" he asked, amazed and relieved that he was able to form words despite the effect of her proximity on him.

Her lips brushed his ear, her scent more intoxicating than their drink. "Can't you guess?"

"Tell me," he whispered, even as he struggled to keep from grabbing her shoulders and claiming her mouth with his.

Her tongue flicked across the top of his ear. He grabbed

the edge of the table and squeezed, willing himself to stay sane.

"I want you to tell me something first," she whispered.

"Vixen," he teased.

She eased forward so he could see more of her face, more of her eyes, dark with passion. Her finger dipped into the drink, and she moved it to her mouth, parting her lips, sucking the liquid from her own finger. Then she dragged her finger casually over her full lower lip, her eyes never leaving his face. Teasing eyes and tempting lips. He wanted to lose himself in those lips. Wanted to lose himself in her.

Devin heard a moan, realized it came from him, and knew the world was reeling beneath him.

Paris slipped her finger back into the drink, but this time, instead of raising it to her own lips, she gently grazed his mouth with her moist fingertip. So tender. So inviting.

Craving a deeper taste, Devin drew her finger into his mouth, rolling his tongue over her flesh, reveling in her sweet flavor. Paris shut her eyes, but Devin didn't need to see those liquid brown pools to know she was aroused.

Just as Devin closed his own eyes, Paris withdrew her finger and shifted so their hips no longer touched. His body lamented as he opened his eyes and saw that she'd slid away. Now she leaned against the table, her gaze locked on him, one finger in her mouth. This time the gesture wasn't seductive. Instead, she was nibbling on a fingernail.

Basic, primal need crashed over him.

Was she having second thoughts? Please, no. She'd already taken him to the brink, and the thought of not having her, not touching her was unbearable. He wanted to keep them in this moment with a desperation he'd never felt before. He needed to let the feeling grow, to explore her finger until he knew every taste, every crevice. And then to do the same with every soft, perfect inch of her.

"What did you want to ask me?" He kept his voice low, willing her back to him.

Her smile was fragile. "I shouldn't...we shouldn't..." Paris took a deep breath, then looked down at the table. Devin could tell she was torn, and he stiffened, waiting for her to decide. Everything he wanted in the universe hinged on which way she would come down.

When she lifted her eyes to meet his, he thought he saw an invitation. Devin relaxed, and the earth continued to spin.

"I wanted to know if you really just wanted to run your hands through my hair." She looked away as she spoke, and his heart swelled at her sudden shyness.

Devin held on to the moment for as long as he dared. He wanted to burn that instant into his memory. The way she looked, magnetic, electric, blazing. Her voice, husky with lust. Her scent, flowers and musk.

He stroked her cheek, his fingertips light enough to feel the fine hairs on her perfect skin. Paris closed her eyes again, her lips slightly parted. He caressed her face, outlined her mouth with his fingertips, stopping finally to cup her chin. When he had taken as much as he could from the moment, he brushed his lips over hers.

"Is that what you've been wanting to do?" he asked.

A sparkle in her eyes. A hint of a smile. She shook her head, *no*.

Before Devin could register confusion, she continued. "No. I wanted to do this."

In one movement, she caught his mouth with her kiss. Bold and deep, the kiss was hungry, devouring, nothing like Devin's sensual tease. This was a full-blown kiss. Torrid, lustful, enthusiastic and unmistakably sexy.

Devin returned her ardor. Her mouth was moist and ready for him, and he explored her with his tongue, even as his hands glided over the curve of her neck and the arch of her back. Despite the awkward position, their bodies fit perfectly.

More. He needed to know the rest of her.

"Maybe it's time I walk you to your room," he said, pulling away just enough to look at her. It was a strain for him to get the words out.

Paris's eyes told him what he wanted to know. "Yeah. Maybe it is."

Hours seemed to pass before they settled the bill and caught the elevator. During that eternity they held hands, not saying a word, electricity arcing between them. "What floor are you on?"

"Thirty-five," she said, punching the number.

"You should have taken a room in the single digits. This elevator's horribly slow. I'm not sure I can wait until thirty-five."

With a gleam in her eye, she looked down at the obvious bulge in the front of his slacks. "No, maybe you can't."

Devin pulled her in front of him, his erection pressing against the thin dress and her soft flesh underneath. "Do you have any idea how much I want you?"

She wriggled against him, her unexpected response thrilling him and almost sending him tumbling over the edge. "I've got a pretty good idea," she said.

He groaned into her hair. "Vicious flirt," he murmured.

The elevator stopped at the sixth floor, and Paris straightened up, placing a safe strip of air between them, as a gray-haired woman stepped on and punched the button for the thirty-second floor. She smiled at Devin and Paris, then turned to face the closed elevator doors.

Devin moved closer behind Paris, clasping her around the waist to keep her from pulling away. He peered at their companion. She seemed unconcerned.

When he felt Paris relax in his arms, Devin conjured a fake cough, and, with cough and motion working together, managed to maneuver Paris's zipper down to her waist without their elevator guest noticing. Paris stiffened but didn't say a word.

Devin laid the palm of his hand against her bare back, fearful that Paris would step away. He'd never done anything this bold, but he felt compelled. Desire controlled him. He felt a hunger to know her completely, body, mind, soul. And a need to be the man she wanted, the type of man who was confident enough to seduce a beautiful woman in an elevator.

For her, he could be that man.

Paris held her back rigid and faced forward like a soldier. But she didn't try to move away, and Devin let his fingers glide up and down the path left by her zipper. She shivered, then leaned back into him, her sigh almost inaudible.

Trailing his fingers up her back, Devin kept his eyes on the gray-haired lady, ready to drop his mission if need be, but still tantalized by the prospect of discovery. He felt the pattern of Paris's spine, traced the gentle curve of her shoulder blade, and found the soft skin under her arm. Her body rose and fell as her breathing became more labored. She was forcing herself to stay in control. He knew, because so was he.

With slow, easy strokes, he caressed her side, up and down under her arm, delighting in her soft skin under his fingers. With each upward stroke, he moved his fingers closer to her front. Paris leaned back, the soft grinding movement of her hips against his groin making him harder than he'd ever been.

When his index finger stroked the soft flesh of her breast, his efforts were rewarded with a small spasm. Was she going crazy? He knew he'd go mad if they didn't soon reach her room.

The elevator stopped at thirty-two, and their impromptu chaperone stepped off. As soon as the elevator doors closed, Paris spun around in his arms, her face flushed.

"Kiss me."

It was an order Devin wouldn't dream of ignoring, and he lost himself in the kiss for the next three floors, lost to everything except the throbbing of his own body and the delicious ambrosia of her mouth under his own.

When they reached Paris's floor, Devin felt a twinge of regret that this woman he was seducing, that was seducing him right back, had absolutely no idea of his name. He started to tell her, then stopped. What was the point? He was from his world, and she was from hers, and never the twain shall meet. She didn't want a Devin O'Malley. Wasn't that obvious? After all, she'd never pressed him for his real name.

Paris wanted Alexander, and Devin had no idea how to change that, how to make her see that he could be everything she wanted.

She wanted Montgomery Alexander, and fortunately for Devin, tonight that's who he was. He wanted tonight with her.

Tomorrow was soon enough to figure out how to get the money, keep Paris and still be Devin O'Malley.

4

"THIS IS IT." Paris indicated her hotel room door with a wave of her hand. She tried to keep her voice normal, casual, but she doubted she succeeded.

Alexander nodded. "So it is."

He stood only inches away, not touching her, but close enough to tease her with the possibility of contact. Part of her wanted him to touch her again, like he had in the elevator, but if he did that, Paris didn't think she could summon the strength not to touch him back. Every part of him. With her fingers, her lips, her tongue. And not just kisses...

After all, wasn't that what she really wanted? Wasn't that why they were standing here in the hallway in front of a room furnished with little more than a bed? She'd been foolishly trying to trick herself into thinking she could survive on only his kisses. But in truth, she wanted all of him. Maybe it was only chemistry between them, but that was okay. After all, she didn't want or need any ties to this man. Just one night of passion to savor forever.

She imagined Alexander, stretched out naked on that king-size bed, holding his hand out, beckoning her to come to him. Urging her to make love to him all night. Just like he did in her fantasies.

The possibility sent her blood rushing.

Anticipation. An old ketchup commercial skittered through her head. *I'm giddy, smitten and starstruck.*

"Are you going to invite me in?" His soft words brought her back to the moment. From the husky tone of his voice, Paris knew he wasn't worried the answer would be "no."

"Sure," she said, then slipped the card key through the slot and watched as the light turned from red to green. Green for go. Green for no holds barred, damn the torpedoes, and all that jazz.

As her hand paused on the door handle, she realized that the etiquette of the situation eluded her. The Fates willing, she was about to sleep with a man she *technically* didn't know all that well—not a normal happening for her.

But he was Alexander. And with Alexander, Paris had no qualms. She may have only met him a few hours ago, but she'd known him all her life.

Girl, you are so losing it.

She ran her free hand through her hair, pulling the curls up and away from her face. What on earth was she doing? He *wasn't* Alexander, and she wasn't going to sleep with him. Adventure in fiction was fine and dandy. But it had no place in her real life. *You are not going to make love with him.* She needed to keep reminding herself of that. For some reason, she kept forgetting.

For some reason? Please. She had good reasons. Lots of them. Like that he was hotter than sin and so very close.

Still, no matter how much she wanted it to be true, he wasn't the man she'd imagined so many times when she was alone in her bed. He couldn't be.

She stressed the point, trying to mentally drive it home. He couldn't be Alexander, because Alexander didn't exist. And this man, the one standing behind her who had almost burned up the elevator with her, was not—repeat, not—her dream man.

She needed to call this off, run for shelter, before it was too late.

Unfortunately, her body wasn't really keen on this new call-it-off plan. Her body wanted to do the kinds of things people did behind hotel room doors.

Her body didn't even care that she didn't know his real name. But what was in a name, really? Especially when the chemistry was so potent. When she melted at his touch. When every thought in her head evaporated under the spell of him.

She sighed. Maybe he really was Alexander.

Or maybe she was trying really hard to think up a justification for sleeping with him.

"Paris?"

She looked up, taking in his bad-boy-turned-corporate-exec good looks that practically oozed sex. The silk tie was loose and his first two buttons were undone, revealing a smattering of gold hair. His eyes glittered, intent on watching her. A smile played at his lips, and Paris thought of the wolf and Red Riding Hood. *The better to eat you with.*

Oh my.

Paris was having a hard time remembering why they were still standing in the doorway. "Um?"

His gaze darted to the partially opened door. "Do I need to guess the password?"

"What?" Paris said, then realized she was blocking his path. "Oh. Sorry."

She stepped into the narrow hallway leading to the main area of the room, then stopped cold. The bed loomed about nine feet away, illuminated by the one reading lamp the maid had left on.

The course of the evening suddenly seemed more real.

And appealing? She paused to consider, but her hormones rushed to answer. *You bet.*

Common sense stepped up to the plate. Just because the room had a bed did not mean they had to put it to good use.

Alexander must have picked up on her hesitation. "Second thoughts?"

"No," she blurted, her hormones beating her pesky common sense into submission. Then she felt herself blush, embarrassed by her quick response. "I mean, please, come in."

Paris wanted to roll her eyes at her awkward eagerness. She couldn't have been any less subtle if she'd ripped her dress off and thrown herself into his arms right then and there. That might be what she wanted to do, but such bold tactics lacked the proper panache. Besides, she was too much of a chicken.

And you're not sleeping with him anyway, remember?

She sighed. Somehow, she kept forgetting that tiny detail.

As he stepped past her toward the bed, their arms brushed, sending enough current surging between them to set the building on fire. Could have, but didn't. Instead, all that energy, all that heat, centered in her stomach and her knees. Just one touch and he'd made her go weak.

Feigning nonchalance, she leaned gratefully against the wall. Her bare back pressed against the smooth, cool paint that didn't even begin to lessen the red-hot passion pounding through her.

He was standing there, right in front of her, so hot he should be burning a hole in the floor. So close Paris could feel his breath, could almost hear his heartbeat.

This amazing hunk of fantasy material was there for her. What a coup. She was privy to a sexual coup. But she was pretty sure she wasn't the one calling the shots. He'd turned her on, mixed her up when she needed to concentrate. She needed to keep her head on straight, needed to strengthen her resolve before he destroyed her defenses without even saying a word.

"I'm not going to make love with you," she blurted, as she sat back on the bed. Immediately she wanted to take it back, but couldn't very well do that. Not without admitting how much his nearness was messing with her head. And with the rest of her.

She looked up at him, expecting to see shock or disappointment. Instead, a smile tugged at the corner of his mouth. "Thanks for letting me know." He looked amused, damn him. Well, he wouldn't look nearly so confident when he realized how determined she was.

"I mean it. No sex."

"I believe you."

"You do?" She frowned. She knew she shouldn't be disappointed with his easy agreement, but she couldn't help it. Alexander wouldn't give up so easily, not if he really wanted her. Alexander was too much of a rogue.

Unless this man was just playing it cool, planning to lower her defenses for a sneak attack. *That* would be very Alexanderish.

He kneeled casually in front of the minibar. "Nightcap?"

"I'm...yes. Please."

Then again, perhaps he was a gentleman and not a rogue at all. She shook her head to clear her muddled thoughts. This man and Alexander were all mixed up in her head.

He popped the cork on a miniature bottle of champagne and poured them both a glass. "How about talking? Is that safe territory?"

Talking? Talking was fine. Kissing would be even better. Kissing fell within her boundaries. But she couldn't really say so without sounding desperate. "What do you want to talk about?"

"You're a writer, right?"

She nodded, wary.

He moved closer and passed her a glass of champagne. His fingers grazed over hers, intimate and purposeful, and any remaining doubts about his desire for her vanished in a puff.

"I thought maybe you'd be interested in an intellectual evening. We could discuss literature."

"Literature?" She didn't believe him for a second, but neither could she guess what he was up to.

"Maybe Victorian-era erotic literature?" His voice had changed, it was lower, rougher. Suggestive.

A trill coursed up her spine. How easy for him to reduce her to quakes and quivers. "I...I don't really know anything about it."

"No? Too bad. How about kissing?" His eyes bore into her without blinking, his desire obvious but still unspoken. She licked her dry lips and looked at the floor.

"Kissing?" she repeated stupidly, unable to think of anything else to say. What had seemed like safe territory only a moment ago suddenly seemed dangerous. Wonderfully appealing, but undeniably dangerous.

Her legs wobbled and the wall no longer seemed capable of holding her up. She stumbled to the bed and sat on the edge, her hands folded primly in her lap, a reminder of what she wasn't going to do with him.

"I thought we could talk about kissing. Is that okay?"

She nodded, not trusting herself to speak. But he could talk all night about kissing if he wanted. That wouldn't break any rules.

Talk? Hell, he could kiss her all night.

He lowered himself onto the bed next to her, close enough that his taut thigh muscles pressed against her. She focused on taking nice, normal breaths. But the more she tried to ignore his heat against her, the more flustered she became.

When he leaned back on the bed, she hesitated to look at him. "It's too hard to talk sitting up next to each other. I promise I don't bite."

She drew a steadying breath and turned her head. He was lounging behind her, propped up on one elbow. He patted the space in front of him. "Come on." Then he grinned, slow and self-assured. "Unless you don't trust yourself with me."

As a matter of fact, she didn't. Not one bit. But she probably shouldn't mention that. She leaned back and scooted up the bed until her face was even with his. She had to admit it was a much better position for talking. It was a much better position for kissing, too. How convenient.

"Now, about kissing." With one fingertip, he traced her lower lip. Her pulse throbbed and she tried to steady her breathing. "Did you know that some people think kissing is more intimate than sex?"

A small sound of interest was the most she could manage.

"There are times when I think that's right," he said, flashing her a lazy grin. His finger teased her lip, then slid inside her mouth to graze the top of her teeth. She closed her eyes, fighting to keep from closing her lips around his finger.

"Not that I'm knocking sex, mind you," he murmured. "I certainly can't deny the intimacy of being naked next to a woman who makes your heart pound as it's never done before, sheathing yourself in her, filling her up, taking her places she's never been and watching her skin flush when she finds satisfaction."

Paris squirmed on the bed, her thighs pressed tight together to try and forestall the liquid urgency that he was creating inside her. She lost the battle with his finger, and closed her lips over him, suckling, hoping that giving in just a little bit would douse the flames that were beginning to consume her.

Gently, he pulled his finger from her mouth. She heard herself whimper.

"But a kiss, a kiss can be sweet and gentle. Or hard and desperate. A kiss is fast and hot and deep, or slow and lingering. A kiss is sharing breath and soul."

Something soft brushed her lips. When his evening beard tickled her cheek, she realized he'd brushed her mouth with a kiss. "Tell me what you think about kissing," he whispered.

She quaked, imagining his lips on hers, his breath mixed with hers. A piece of his soul. And she so wanted to see into his core. She needed to know if he could really be the man she'd dreamed of.

"Paris?"

She opened her eyes. "Just one kiss." Her voice sounded thick, more sultry than she could ever remember.

His eyes darkened. Then Paris saw the hint of a smile. She heard his breath coming as uneven as her own. With a low groan, he pulled her across the satiny bedspread into his arms.

Her breasts pressed hard against his chest, her nipples painfully tight. He took her bottom lip in his mouth and sucked, drawing her blood through her veins with every infinitesimal increase in pressure.

Wriggling closer, she maneuvered her leg over his

thigh, needing to feel him pressed tight against her, wanting to feel the evidence of his arousal against her belly.

His ministrations on her lip continued, and she moaned for him, closing her eyes and balling the material of his shirt in her tight fist as she struggled not to beg him for more.

Desperate, she crushed herself against him and opened her mouth, silently urging him inside her. He played with her mouth, teasing, sucking, nipping, but never entering.

When he drew away, she shivered from the cool air that replaced his hot breath. His attention had made her lips full and swollen. Raw with kisses. And she wanted more. Opening her eyes, she saw him smiling at her, his own mouth moist.

"Please..." She could only manage one word, but that was all it took. He cupped her face and pulled her to him, his mouth claiming hers, fast, hard, primitive and completely satisfying. Their tongues fought a timeless battle of male and female, lust and desire.

She writhed against him, wanting a satisfaction his kisses alone wouldn't bring.

He released his claim on her mouth. "Paris. Oh, Paris..."

The poor man sounded almost wounded. She'd never imagined herself capable of causing such a reaction, but she knew well enough it was real. She brushed her lips across his. "Yes?"

"You're killing me. I can't keep kissing you, touching you, and not be deep inside you." Raw and gravelly with desire, his voice confirmed his words.

"Oh. I..." She could barely force words past the haze of passion. Right then, all she knew was that she hungered for him. She'd made up rules, silly rules. But her body answered to a different law, and her rules now seemed best ignored. Or broken.

"Paris, what do you want?" His murmur stroked and enticed her, turning the rivers of lust coursing through her into white water rapids.

The space within his arms seemed to shrink. Her eyes locked with his, knowing that if he could see into her heart, he would see only passion.

For years, her only adventure had been in her books. For one night, she wanted to live that adventure. With him. With Alexander.

"You," she whispered. "Tonight I want you." Maybe it was just lust, but she wanted him inside her with a desperation she'd never felt before. She might regret it in the morning, but tonight she needed him. It didn't matter that he couldn't really be Alexander. Hadn't he told her that, just for tonight, he was? And he had to be...

He had to be her dream man. After all, who besides Alexander could make her feel this way?

DEVIN COULDN'T TAKE his eyes off her.

Paris had said she wanted him—had said it out loud—and he intended to make love to her like no other man ever could. More erotic, more sensual, more thrilling than any lover she'd ever had.

Or had ever fantasized about.

With slow, torturous movements he grazed his hand along her thigh, her hose silky under his fingers. He watched the desire on her flushed face as his fingers moved casually up her leg. When his thumb grazed soft skin instead of silk, she shivered, and he stopped, surprised.

"Stockings?"

She nodded, her tongue flicking across her lips.

"Oh, sweetheart. I knew you were sexy under that dress. I didn't imagine this."

His finger skimmed the edge of the stocking until he found the snap of her garter. He moaned and took a second to fight for control, pressing himself closer to her.

"I didn't think panty hose fit a special occasion. The publisher's party, I mean." She smiled at him, soft and feminine and a little shy. "I didn't realize quite how special the night would turn out to be."

Her innocent, sweet words and halo of golden curls contrasted with the naughty lingerie and the heated arousal of her skin under his touch. The effect was honest and feminine and breathtaking.

Devin wanted her even more. He hadn't thought such a thing possible.

"Any more incredible surprises I should know about?"

Wordlessly, she shook her head as his fingers fumbled over the snap. He eased her stocking down and off, then traced his finger back up her leg, along the outside of her thigh to the edge of her panties.

When his finger slipped under the elastic, her breathing became ragged and she closed her eyes. He teased her a little, tracing the edge of her panties, knowing she wanted him to go farther, but not quite willing to do that yet. Not until she was ready. Not until she was desperate.

When he pulled his hand away, she whimpered, but he kissed her into silence as his hand moved higher, a light tease on the outside of her dress, over her hard nipples, to her shoulder.

He fingered the straps. "If you don't want me to rip this off you, I suggest you slide out of it."

The thought had a certain appeal, and for a moment he considered just grabbing her dress and tugging, leaving her surprised and naked against him.

Primitive, yes. Satisfying, absolutely.

But probably not a good idea.

She shifted just enough to let him ease the dress off her, leaving her naked except for panties, her garter belt and one stocking.

Damn, she was gorgeous. "You're beautiful."

An adorable blush painted her already flushed cheeks.

"It's true," he insisted, but she just grabbed the edge of the bedspread and pulled it over her.

He grinned. No way she was getting away with that.

"Come on, sweetheart, I want to see more of you." He took her hand and urged her to push the bedspread away. Her easy agreement and shy smile told him the compliments embarrassed her—not their intimate activities.

Good. The evening promised to get a lot more intimate. As for the compliments, well, eventually she'd get used to those. And if not, that blush was damned alluring.

He positioned her so that she was sitting at the foot of the bed, her feet flat on the floor, her hands behind her so that her shoulders were back and her chest was out. Her breasts rose and fell erratically with her ragged breathing. Her tight nipples begged to be kissed.

His own breath came just as choppy. Just watching her, without touching her, was sending his control spiraling away into oblivion.

From her breasts, his eyes moved down to her tiny waist, so small he could probably encircle it with his hands. Next, her round hips, still clothed in the silk panties he'd already explored. By the time his eyes lingered on the small patch of black material just between her thighs, he felt as if he would burst out of his tailored slacks.

Because the material was dark and her thighs were almost closed, he couldn't tell if she was wet for him. But he imagined he already knew the answer to that. Her breathing, her heat, her scent, her eyes. Everything about her screamed that she was as aroused as he was.

Just knowing that excited him, made him anxious to see what other feelings he could coax out of her, how crazy he could make her before the sun came up.

How crazy he could make himself.

"Please," she whispered.

"Please what?"

"Touch me."

Her words cut straight to his groin. *Yes, oh, yes.*

He knelt in front of her and ran his tongue along the top of her remaining stocking, lingering over her feminine taste. He stopped just long enough to look at her. "Touch you like that?"

She opened her mouth, but didn't answer.

He teased her with his thumb, leaving her skin tight and hot. When he traced the edge of her panties with his forefinger, sliding his finger just under the material, she bit her lip.

"Like that, maybe?"

"Yes," Paris moaned, her voice hoarse with passion, "like that."

He continued his erotic exploration, his tongue tasting the inside of her thigh as his finger teased her, always just out of reach of where he knew she wanted. Sweet torment for her.

And for him. He wanted to be inside her, exploring her silky folds. Touching her. Kissing her.

"Don't stop..." she begged.

Devin's breath caught and he smiled, more than happy to oblige.

Bang, bang, bang. The pounding filtered through Paris's muddled thoughts, and the moment shattered around her.

She bolted upright, pulling away from all the wonderful things Alexander was doing to her body. He stared back at her, his breathing just as uneven as hers.

She looked at the clock. Two forty-eight in the morning.

"Room service?" he whispered.

"We didn't order anything." The pounding repeated. "Should I answer it?"

Alexander traced his finger up the side of her arm. "Do you have to?"

"Paris?" Rachel's voice spilled into the room.

Paris cringed, sure that she was blushing. "It's Rachel." She looked at Alexander. "I *do* have to answer it."

"It's the middle of the night. Does she do this often?"

"Paris!" Rachel's voice had shifted from urgent to annoyed.

"Coming," called Paris, managing a shrug for Alexander's sake as she slid off the bed and began hustling into a terry-cloth robe she'd left hanging over an armchair. "Do what? Girl talk after hours? Not often. Maybe she wants a shoulder to cry on. Or someone to do tequila shots with."

Alexander pitched her dress and shoes into the closet. "Don't let her cry for too long. I have plans for that shoulder." He trailed his index finger over the shoulder in question.

Paris smiled. "That's a deal." She turned toward the door. "One second, Rachel. I was just in the bathroom."

"Well, hurry. I've got some amazing news." Rachel's voice was laced with excitement.

Paris looked at Alexander. "Wait for me in your room," she whispered.

His face registered only confusion. "Where?"

Paris steered him toward the connecting room. She grabbed the key off the top of the television, and opened the door.

"Whose room is this?"

"Yours," she said immediately, then, "I mean Alexander's. I always take two rooms. One for me, and one for Alexander. Otherwise, people might talk."

"Paris, I—"

She cut him off. "Please, hurry. I'm already teetering on mortification, here."

"That doesn't even compare to what I'm teetering on the brink of," he shot back with a grin.

Paris shook her head. "Men. Might I remind you that you're the one who gets to hide while I get to be totally embarrassed in front of my best friend?"

He surprised her with a gentle kiss on the tip of her nose. "Don't be embarrassed. You deserve this night." He pulled the door shut behind him before she had a chance to respond.

Easy for him to say. Paris agreed that she deserved every moment spent with her Alexander. But now her best friend was gearing up to give her the teasing of a lifetime, laced with a liberal number of I-told-you-so's. And there was no solace in hoping Rachel wouldn't figure out what had been going on. No matter how hard Paris tried to keep it a secret, the odds were that somehow, someway, Rachel would realize what Paris had been on the brink of doing with...*who?*

She stopped dead, as reality took this opportunity to conk her on the head. Was she actually about to sleep with a man whose name she didn't even know? What was she thinking?

And what about Rachel? Paris would never hear the end of it from Rachel if she didn't know his name. She lunged for the connecting door and tried the knob. Locked.

Rachel pounded again. "Paris, for crying out loud, the Queen doesn't take this long."

"Coming," squeaked Paris, cringing when she realized how nervous she sounded. A quick glance around the room revealed nothing that would hint at her recent extracurricular activities. Taking a breath, she hurried to the front of the room and unlatched the door.

Rachel burst in the second the lock released.

"Finally! I've been trying to call you."

Paris shrugged. "I stayed out late." She hurried to change the subject. "What's the big rush?"

"You'll never believe it, not in a million years." She rubbed her fingers against her thumb. "Know what this is? Cash, moola, greenbacks. Money for you, and money for me."

"Either it's too late or you're not making any sense."

"And it's going to be so easy, I promise," Rachel rushed on.

Paris was on the verge of shaking her friend. "*What's* going to be so easy? What are you talking about?"

Rachel grimaced. "Of course there is one hitch." She held up her hand as if Paris had moved to protest, when in fact Paris was standing completely still, dumbstruck by Rachel's frenetic rambling. "But it's minor, really. We can work it out."

"Rachel, focus for me here. Work *what* out?"

"You got his number, right?"

"Whose number?" asked Paris, even as a queer feeling in her stomach suggested that she already knew the answer.

"From the party. Alexander. He's essential. We absolutely have to have him."

A SMUG GRIN covered about ninety percent of Rachel's face.

"You're kidding me, right?" Paris asked, for about the thirtieth time.

Rachel shook her head. "I told you, it's true."

"A three-book deal? Hardback? This is so...so... amazing. I don't even know what to say." She flung herself at Rachel and kissed her on the cheek. The two women linked arms and swung each other around the room, letting loose war whoops every now and then for good measure.

Paris let go of Rachel, scrambled onto the bed and did a little jig before falling backward onto the mattress. "You realize what this means, don't you?"

Rachel smiled. "Yes, but you're going to tell me anyway."

Paris sat up. "Darn right. It means that after this deal I'll have enough money to live on while I finish *Distant Passages.*"

Rachel shrugged. "If that's what you want to do."

"Of course that's what I want. It's what I've always talked about."

"Always? When we were little girls you wanted to write about spies and secret codes and hidden passageways. Seems to me you're already doing that."

Paris frowned. "Things change. When we were little you wanted to have a big house with a wraparound porch and a swing. That doesn't sound like any place I've ever seen in Manhattan. And I don't see you getting the urge to move back to Texas."

"That's different. I don't want a house like that anymore. Really." Paris thought about arguing, but decided it wasn't the time. "And wild horses couldn't get me back to

Braemer," Rachel added. "But you, on the other hand, do want to keep writing the Montgomery Alexander books."

"What I want is to write *Distant Passages*, sell it, and be respectable." For a brief moment, Paris wondered if the forceful tone of her voice was meant to convince Rachel, or herself.

"Well, at least you'll have the clout to sell—" Rachel cut herself off before finishing. "Sorry," she added.

"No, I won't have the clout to sell it. *I'm* not Montgomery Alexander. But at least as his manager I can convince Brandon to take a look at it. And maybe Alexander's fabulous agent can help shop it around."

Rachel nodded. "Sounds like a plan. After all, he's got the most amazing agent, if I do say so myself." She winked at Paris. "But rumor has it his manager is a little loopy."

"Go ahead," Paris laughed, "taunt all you want. Nothing's going to get a rise out of me today."

"Nothing?"

"Nope."

"You're sure?" Rachel pressed.

Something in Rachel's voice caught Paris's attention. "What are you worried about? It's about him, isn't it?"

"Did you get his number? Do you know when he works at the pub? You got his real name, right? We have to get in touch with him."

"No, he owns it, no, and why?" Paris crossed her arms over her chest and waited for Rachel's explanation.

"It's not a big deal, really," said Rachel, her voice lyrical and soothing.

Paris knew better. "What's not a big deal?"

"Just-that-they-want-Alexander-to-do-a-book-tour." The words tumbled over each other like toddlers in a tiny tots' gymnastics class. She took a breath. "A short tour.

More a publicity jaunt than a book tour. Ellis Chapman was really impressed. Said Alexander's got charisma. And he thinks we can increase female readership if he does some public appearances and talk shows."

Paris imagined Alexander's chiseled features accented by his enigmatic smile and come-hither eyes. Yes, Ellis had a point.

The import of Rachel's words struck home. "Television? Interview shows?"

Rachel nodded.

"You agreed to this?"

"Well, I said I had to check with you, of course, but that I didn't think it would be a problem."

"Not a problem? Rachel, it's a huge problem. How are we supposed to pull it off? Alexander's given about fifty on-line and written interviews over the last few years. This guy's not going to have any idea what Alexander's said in the past. He'll forget something and screw up, and the gig'll be over."

"So, other than the interview shows, you're okay with the idea?"

Trapped. Paris was trapped like a rat. She tried to back out slowly without getting even more entangled in barbed wire. "No, it's not okay. I just latched on to the first and biggest of about five-million problems with this plan."

On the one hand Rachel had just created the perfect opportunity to spend more time with Alexander. More time doing exactly what they'd been doing. And more.

But on the other hand—the one that still had a grip on sanity and her career—Rachel had just upped the ante on Paris's whole scheme. Unless Alexander was one-hundred-percent perfect all of the time, someone would surely catch on.

"No book tour, no contract. No contract, no nest egg to support you."

"If *Dearest Enemy, Deadly Friend* continues to do okay, I bet they'll offer another contract."

Rachel shrugged. "Maybe."

Paris glared at Rachel, irritated that her friend was right. For years, Paris had been telling herself that she wanted to retire the Montgomery Alexander books and turn to serious fiction. The kind that got reviewed on PBS, won obscure literary prizes and could justify a visiting professor position at some prestigious university. All the trappings of upper-strata respectability necessary to be a card-carrying member of the Sommers clan.

So far the money wasn't enough to keep her in food and shelter while she worked on *Distant Passages*. She needed a job lined up in case the book was a huge flop. Of course, she could go back to being a lawyer full-time to make money, but the hours were too intense if she wanted to get any serious writing done.

Now someone had dangled a carrot in front of her nose. She could finish her first important book and get started on another while she still had the security of steady income from Montgomery Alexander. Even with the risks, she'd be a fool to turn down the opportunity.

She glanced at the door to Alexander's room, thinking about the delicious perks that would go along with the arrangement. After only one night, Paris wasn't ready to blurt out her undying love, but neither did she want him to just walk away. She at least wanted to know his name.

Somewhere between the bar and her room, sometime between the flirting and the kisses, she'd begun to want more from this Alexander than just one wild night of adventure. She wanted to go out, maybe eat dinner and see a movie. Heck, she wanted sex. Normal life stuff.

Of course, her life was rarely normal. And it seemed to be getting more abnormal by the minute. Alexander might not fit into her long-term plan, but in the meantime, if she couldn't have normalcy, she'd take this.

"I'll do it."

"Yes!" Rachel punched the sky and whooped. "Okay, so how do we get in touch with our man Alexander? Do you have a phone number?"

"Call him? Now? What's the rush? Go home and we'll track him down tomorrow."

Rachel shook her head, sending her hair flying. "No, no. You don't understand. You have to leave the day after tomorrow."

Paris blinked and clutched the edge of the bed. "What? How?"

"I told you, it's a short tour. Do you remember Madame Marasky, the one who writes all those psychic detective books?" Paris nodded, not sure what the funny old gypsy woman had to do with Alexander. "Well, she lives in California, so the publicity folks had her booked on a ton of morning radio programs and a few television talk shows. Then she scheduled book signings all up and down the coast. That's the first leg. Then she was booked to go to Las Vegas for the book and media convention. Only a couple of weeks, but heavy on the public relations." She paused for a second before rushing on. "Oh, and there's even a few days in Texas. Maybe we can get your dad to throw one of his killer parties."

Paris rubbed her temples. Maybe it was the late hour, but Rachel still wasn't making any sense. "What does this have to do with me or my dad?"

"Madame Marasky's having gallbladder surgery. You're getting her itinerary. You and Alexander. But you have to be on the ten o'clock flight to Los Angeles the day after tomorrow." She looked at her watch. "Actually, tomorrow. Because today already is tomorrow, so the day after tomorrow would be too late."

The news settled over Paris. A book tour. With radio and television. Wow. She sucked in a deep breath. She just needed to round up her imposter.

Rachel's eyes drifted to Paris's robe. "Throw on some jeans and let's run down to his bar. Maybe we can catch him cleaning up or something."

Paris glanced down at the pattern on the carpet, willing the blood to leave her cheeks and go back to other parts of her body where it belonged. "Um. I—"

She couldn't finish. Rachel was her best friend. And best friends make the most notorious teasers.

"What?" As Rachel stared at Paris, the question in her eyes transformed into curiosity, then speculation.

Paris hurried to jump in, before Rachel could leap to a conclusion even more bawdy than the truth. "We don't have to go to his bar."

"Oh? Do tell."

Paris hadn't seen Rachel looking so interested in anything since they'd watched the "Introduction to our Bodies" filmstrip in sixth grade health class.

Without thinking, Paris turned toward the connecting door. Rachel's gaze followed, her expression blank. Then she looked at the bed and the tangled bedclothes. Paris knew the second her friend figured it out.

"He's next door—" Paris blurted out.

"I can't believe you didn't tell me—" Rachel said at the same time.

They both laughed.

"You're the one who said I should," Paris reminded Rachel.

"Well, yes, but I never thought you'd actually listen. Lord knows, even I hardly ever follow my own advice."

"If it's any consolation, nothing's happened. Yet. *Somebody* interrupted before we got to the main attraction."

Rachel actually had the decency to look embarrassed. But just slightly. "At least I interrupted for a good reason, right?"

Paris pretended to pout. "Well, your news *could* have waited until morning."

Rachel laughed. "If it had occurred to me that there was even the remotest possibility that you would be doing what you were thinking about doing, I would have waited. And waited. And waited." She winked. "And then I'd have waited a little more."

Images of the way the evening *didn't* turn out flashed through Paris's mind. "Oh, oh my gosh."

Rachel's eyes widened. "What?"

Paris ran her hands through her hair, trying to avoid the reality that was creeping toward her. "I was actually going to go to bed with a man I'd just met."

"No, no, no. A *cute* man you'd just met."

"Not cute. Gorgeous."

Rachel nodded. "I'll give you that one. And you have a lot in common."

"Well, yes. We have *him* in common."

Rachel raised an eyebrow. "And you like him, right?"

Paris remembered the way his hands had raked over her body, hearing again all the things he'd whispered in her ear. Her body flushed with the memory. He'd been right there for her. Touchable. Kissable. *Real.*

She knew the smile she flashed Rachel was one of complete satisfaction. "Oh, yeah. He's wonderful."

Trouble was, she didn't exactly know who *he* was.

5

DEVIN FELT LIKE a grinning idiot, unable to wipe the smile off his face. Paris completed him, made him feel like a whole person. They'd been together almost nonstop since the party began, and he still hadn't soaked up enough of her. No woman had ever affected him so much or so quickly.

He fought the urge to burst through the connecting door, interrupt her meeting and whisk Paris away to some white sand beach. Anyplace but here, where they each had their predetermined roles to play.

But that was impossible. In a few minutes, Rachel would leave, and Paris would knock on the door. Devin would go in, they'd make love, then morning would come, along with orange juice, muffins and the moment of truth.

And what then?

Devin stood in front of the mirror, challenging his reflection to come up with a way to get the money he needed without scamming Paris. His reflection failed.

All you have to do is remind her of what a great Montgomery Alexander you make and what a huge favor you did for her. You hand Paris her checkbook and tell her to write. And if she doesn't, you drop the bad news. Simple.

Devin wasn't sure if the voice in his head belonged to his father, Jerry, or himself. All he knew was that whoever was speaking was going to be sorely disappointed.

Then just forget the money and stay with her.

Now that was an intriguing idea. Everything about Paris fascinated him—and not just sexually. Something about her recharged him. Her wit, her gentleness, her mystery. Even the odd dichotomy between her wild-ride books and her staid and proper family. This was a woman with a lot of layers. And he wanted to peel away each layer until he knew all of her.

The heavy connecting-room door drew his attention. He could burn it, break it, somehow get through it. No problem.

If only that door was the only thing between him and Paris.

Fat chance, buddy. You've got some serious competition.

That was an understatement. If he had any hope of something developing between him and Paris, he'd have to compete against her fantasy, his performance of her dream man, and the public image of a suave, sophisticated, mysterious author. He'd have to compete against Montgomery Alexander.

Devin groaned. He didn't stand a chance.

He took a tentative step toward the door to the hallway, urging his leaden feet to do the right thing and carry him away.

Paris had been willing to give herself to Montgomery Alexander, not Devin O'Malley. The man she wanted to make love with was suave, sophisticated, a witty raconteur, a man who could dine at the White House or in a foxhole. Montgomery Alexander could probably quote Yeats while smuggling encrypted messages across the Serbian border.

Contrast that with Devin O'Malley, for whom a good week meant no screwups with payroll or inventory, no employees calling in sick, and no Carmen and his mob cretins breathing down his neck. Hardly the epitome of the man Paris wanted.

He was stuck in a dilemma. He couldn't go through with his blackmail scheme and still look himself in the mirror. But neither could he stay with her, pretending that two such different people actually had a chance.

So he left, slipping into the hallway and pushing the button for the elevator before he could change his mind. All the while he half hoped she'd poke her head out the door and catch him. But of course she didn't. It wasn't meant to be.

The down-arrow lit up, and Devin stepped in, fighting back memories of touching Paris in this very elevator just a few hours earlier. He swore he could still smell her perfume.

Like a vertical fade in an old-fashioned movie, the door slid shut, cutting off his view of the door to Paris's hotel room. How fitting. End of the scene, end of that chapter of his life.

He wondered when she would realize he'd left. Would she be hurt? Angry? Relieved? He hoped not. As much as he didn't want to hurt her, he couldn't believe that she'd be happy to find him gone. Their time together had been special, almost magical. For himself, he needed to hold fast to the belief that she thought so, too.

Devin leaned against the polished wood panels of the elevator, fixed in place by the strong grip of hesitation. He fought the urge to get off at the next floor, race back up the stairs and pull her into his arms.

Don't even think about it, Devie-boy. No, he had done the right thing by walking away. Best to make a clean break, even if the leaving pained him.

He caught the tail end of an idea and stood a little straighter, his hand heading for the Stop button.

Maybe he should tell her the truth. Perhaps the best thing to do would be to lay it all on the line and invite her out for a proper date. After all, when he started this scheme he'd had no idea how he would end up feeling about her.

"You're pathetic, Dev," he whispered, dropping his hand. He was trying to justify a reason to stay based on the strength of his own feelings. But what about Paris?

She was an up-and-coming author with a carved-in-stone image of the man she wanted. She didn't have any room in her life for a pub owner mortgaged to his eyeballs and scurrying to satisfy a debt he couldn't pay.

Devin couldn't be Montgomery Alexander forever. Sooner or later, he'd have to be just Devin. And as much as he wished it weren't true, just Devin wasn't the man Paris wanted.

Their short-lived affair was over before it even had a chance to start.

Except.

The elevator thudded to a halt in the lobby and Devin pushed the thought away. Even his dad would know better than to bet on Paris sauntering into Devin's bar of her own free will, hoping to continue where they'd left off. Stuff like that only happened in fiction, an area Devin no longer had anything to do with.

"HE'S A CREEP."

"Paris," Rachel chided, rolling down her window to let some fresh air into the stale taxi.

"No, it's true. He's a creep and I'm an idiot." Paris kept her voice at a monotone, using no more emotion than a store-special announcer at the local mega-mart. "I should have known from the first moment. It's his eyes. They're shifty."

"His eyes are *not* shifty."

No, his eyes are gorgeous. Deep and inviting.

"Maybe they shift just a little," Paris insisted, gunning for a squabble, but Rachel wasn't going to be baited. The problem, of course, was that Paris didn't want him to be a creep, and didn't believe that he was one, not really, even though he'd engaged in some very creep-like behavior. But ranting felt good, and Paris intended to wallow in it.

Rachel flopped against the soiled upholstery, then crossed her legs in an I'm-in-control sort of way. Paris knew better. Rachel usually made balancing on the edge of taxicab seats an art, careful not to let her typically chic outfits get more mussed up than absolutely necessary. Today, however, Rachel was practically hugging the tattered back seat.

"What are you so upset about?" Paris demanded. "I'm the one who almost boffed some lunatic with a slick come-on line."

Rachel grimaced and looked out the window. Paris gave up. Rachel wasn't going to say a word until she calmed down.

Fat chance that would happen anytime soon. Paris had been indulging in a grab bag of emotions since about three-thirty in the morning. It was now one in the afternoon. Except for a four-hour nap between five and nine, Paris had been bingeing nonstop on self-pity and anger, with a high emphasis on embarrassment. For a woman who usually kept her cool, Paris thought she was doing a heck of a job in the ranting and raving department.

She had to admit, though, it was getting a little old. And all the pouting in the world wouldn't get her the information she really wanted—*why?* Why had he walked away?

Out her window, the Manhattan streets groaned under

the weight of taxis, buses and cars, each moving at a snail's pace, with drivers gesturing wildly to each other in a futile effort to make the traffic move more quickly. Paris didn't mind the delay. The longer it took to get where they were going, the more time she had to prepare to meet *him*.

What *did* annoy Paris was that some secret, almost-buried, traitorous part of her wanted to see him again, to touch him and feel his arms around her. To feel her breath catch and her blood boil the way it had last night.

She leaned her head back against the seat and stared at the roof of the taxi. For six years, she'd lived her life in neat little compartments. Her future had been all planned out, what kind of books she would write, what kind of man she'd marry.

Twenty-four hours ago Paris had total control of her perfect plan. Now chaos had taken over. Her world was swerving out of control. And she didn't like that one bit.

"Rach, maybe I should just tell Chapman everything."

Rachel turned and stared at Paris, her face a mixture of annoyance and concern—an expression that evolved into something even more significant. If she hadn't seen it herself, Paris would never have believed that Rachel could give such an in-depth response without even saying a word.

Paris sighed, drawing out the sound until she noticed the cabdriver eyeing her in the rearview mirror, possibly wondering about her sanity. She was sane, all right. But if she was going to suffer, she was going to do it in style. A little melodrama never hurt anyone.

She shot Rachel an accusatory glare. Usually Rachel was as loyal a friend as Paris could want. But today, instead of helping like agents and best friends were supposed to, Rach was just sitting there like a bump on a log.

"If you don't say something, I really am going to tell."

"Honey, we went over this earlier. You don't want to tell Chapman. Embarrassment, remember? Money? Deal?"

"I can't believe I'm about to beg help from some guy who left me half-naked in a hotel room without even a goodbye note."

"Are you mad at him for leaving, or at yourself for what was going on in your dirty little mind?"

"Whose side are you on?"

"I'm on the side that gets us another book deal."

"Nice. You're a real pal."

Rachel laughed. "Oh, come on, Paris. You're more mad at the situation than you are at him. You practically slept with the guy, something you never do despite all of my urging and coaxing. And now you're embarrassed because the one time you steer from your normal little dull routine, the plan backfires."

There were times when Rachel could be so *right*. It was downright annoying. "It didn't backfire, it exploded. He left. Poof. Picture a big cloud of dust. Then the dust settles, and, golly gee...there's...no...guy."

"Well, he's probably just as embarrassed as you."

Paris doubted that. "How do you figure?"

"He came to the party to meet you. Maybe he fantasized that you'd fall for his Montgomery Alexander routine—"

"So far he's right on the money."

"—but he never *really* believed it," Rachel finished, shooting Paris a do-you-mind look. "And then when you do fall for him, it's like this fantasy come true. First he figured out the secret, and then he seduced the woman of his obsession."

Paris had never been the object of anyone's obsession before, at least that she knew of. "Go on," she urged.

"Well, you're both wrapped up in this fantasy. And you've got great chemistry on top of it."

Paris nodded. No matter what, the chemistry between her and Alexander had crackled.

"So when I knocked and you scooted him off to never-never land, reality probably kicked in. I'll bet he thought you'd be hopping mad once the haze of passion wore off. He probably thought he should get out of there before you had him arrested."

"So you're buying his story that he pulled off the whole thing just to meet me?"

Rachel shrugged. "Sure, why else? He knew all those lines. He's obviously a fan."

Maybe. But something wasn't clicking. Still, what Rachel said about Alexander being embarrassed made some sense. If it had been her shuttled off to the connecting room, maybe reality would have propelled her out of the hotel as well.

"You're probably right," Paris conceded. "Still, it's going to be awkward seeing him again like this." *Awkward and exciting.*

"Thirteen-fifty."

Paris looked at Rachel and then at the cabdriver, who was holding out his hand for the fare. She hadn't noticed when they'd pulled up in front of the pub.

Rachel got to her purse first. "Here."

They slipped out of the cab, and crossed the sidewalk to O'Malley's Pub. A brass placard announced the establishment's hours from four in the afternoon until two in the morning.

"Maybe they're in there doing prep work," Rachel suggested.

Paris nodded, then grabbed the heavy door and pulled. Unlocked, it opened easily. "Here goes nothing," she said, stepping inside with Rachel at her heels.

With three hours left until the bar officially opened, the dim lamplight of the other night had been abandoned in favor of strong, institutional fluorescents. The stale smell of old beer and cigars assaulted Paris, seeming much more pungent than it had during the pub's regular hours, when the odors of alcohol and tobacco had been tempered with music, sweat and fried foods.

The only person in the bar was a lanky fellow squatting on the floor. Earnestly rubbing at a stain on the hardwood planks, he hadn't yet noticed Paris and Rachel. The expression on his face suggested that he'd be happier if the lights were dimmed again, so that the spot he was working so hard to remove would just blend into the shadows.

Paris coughed lightly. The lanky fellow shifted his weight, still concentrating on the stain.

"We ain't open 'til four," he said, without looking up.

"I know. I need to see the owner."

The fellow grunted, as if being interrupted from his chore was the most disruptive thing that had happened to him in ages. He looked up, and Paris saw his eyes widen as he turned from her to Rachel, and then back to Paris.

His mouth hung open as he stared at her.

Paris checked to make sure all her buttons and zippers were fastened. They were. *Have I turned green?*

She opened her mouth to speak, just as the fellow scrambled to stand up. "Oh, it's you. I didn't know. Sorry. What can I get you? Really, anything. It's on the house."

Paris looked at Rachel, who managed to twitch her shoulder and cock one eyebrow in a gesture that left no doubt that she, too, was clueless.

"I'll take a margarita on the rocks," Rachel announced after only a second's hesitation.

Or maybe not so clueless.

"Rachel," snarled Paris, as the fellow loped toward the bar.

"What?" Rachel asked, the picture of innocence. "He asked, and it's rude to turn down your host's invitation."

"Two seconds ago he was kicking us out. Now we're the guests of honor?" Paris lowered her voice, even though it wasn't necessary. The fellow had started the blender, and its grating noise in the empty bar was sufficient to mask their conversation.

Rachel smirked. "From the way he's been looking at you, I'd say you're the guest of honor. I'm just along for the tequila."

Paris was spared having to think of a snappy retort by the sudden silence in the bar.

"Here you go. One margarita." The fellow held up the glass, then set it on the bar.

"It's like a carrot," Rachel mumbled. "He puts it over there, and I'm drawn to it." She headed across the room to the bar. Paris rolled her eyes and followed.

Their de facto host nodded toward Rachel as he looked at Paris. "So, who's she? Your lawyer?"

Odd question. "We did go to law school together, but—"

"Aw, geez, I knew it. I freakin' knew it. I shoulda kept my big mouth shut. He's gonna be up to his armpits in lawyers and cops, and it's all cuz o' me."

Questions ricocheted in Paris mind. Who's going to be in trouble with the lawyers? What did the police have to do with anything? What did *she* have to do with anything? Was the lanky fellow's "he" her Mystery Man? She had a feeling she could place a bet on that one, and have pretty good odds of winning.

One question came to land on her tongue. "Who are you?"

Suddenly all smiles, the fellow slid around the bar to shake her hand. "Jerry. Jerry Mangolini. Wow. What an honor. Meetin' you, I mean. I've read your books. Every one of 'em."

Paris heard Rachel gasp, and considered asking for a sip of the margarita. She was beginning to think she was going to need it. Then again, this was a situation best approached with caution. And a clear head.

"Um, what books are those?"

Jerry nudged her with his shoulder as if they were old friends. "Don't worry. I won't tell. Ironic, ain't it? Me keepin' your secret even though Devin was gonna spill the beans unless, well, you know." He rubbed his thumb and fingers together, the international symbol for money.

Devin. "Devin was—" She couldn't finish the thought.

"—going to blackmail Paris?"

Good ol' Rachel. Always ready to pitch in during a crisis.

"That's why you two are here, right?"

"N—"

"Yes. Of course." Rachel interrupted before Paris could deny having any inkling that the fabulously suave mystery man of her dreams was actually a wolf in Montgomery Alexander clothing.

Overall, the situation stunk.

Jerry nodded. "I'm surprised you found him, him not telling you who he is and all. Guess you musta recognized him from the other day, huh."

"The day when you two figured out my secret identity?"

Jerry cocked a finger at her. "Yeah. You're getting it. A beautiful scheme, really. Worthy of the kind of gigs Devin's pop used to pull." He paused, frowning. "But you might as well lose the lawyer. He didn't go through with it. He told me. Left without getting the money and everything."

"That makes it right?" Paris asked the strange little man.

"Right, not right. Don't really matter. The important thing's that no DA's gonna care about a blackmail scheme wherein no one got blackmailed."

Paris had to agree with the fellow. Even if she were inclined to prosecute, no district attorney would care.

"Besides," continued Jerry, "he had his reasons. Good reasons. Twenty thousand of 'em."

"What?" Rachel asked.

"Gambling debt," Jerry announced. "His—"

"Hello, Paris."

Paris spun around, and there he was—Alexander, Devin, whatever the heck he called himself. Gone was the deep brown hair from the night before. Now damp golden waves framed his face, as if he'd just showered away the remnants of Alexander. But the change didn't reduce his sex appeal at all.

Her first impulse was not to accuse him of trying to rip her off. Not to yell at him for leaving her in a lurch. Not to scream at him for using her. Not to slap him for playing Russian roulette with her heart.

No, her traitorous heart wanted to kiss him, touch him, be near him.

And that was what really made her angry.

THE LOOK ON HER FACE put a quick end to Devin's fantasy that they were going to ride off into the sunset together. Damn, but she looked sexy when she was ticked off.

"Gambling debt," she whispered. "You were going to blackmail me so that you could pay off a gambling debt?"

Her voice rose from a low tremor to a high shrill. Devin cringed. This was definitely not happily ever after.

So much for her rushing over to confess true love, or at least serious lust. How did that saying go? Be careful what you wish for, you just might get it.

"Paris, it wasn't like that." He hoped a soothing voice would keep her from crossing the line into hysterics.

"Wasn't it? What was it like? Some innocent, starstruck fan just wanting to get close to me?" She stomped her foot, and glanced over the bar. Fortunately, the ashtrays were in the dishwasher. Had one been handy, no doubt she'd have hurled it.

She snorted. "Can you believe I fell for that one? I actually thought you were interested in me. Bet you and your buddies'll have a million laughs over that one."

Devin wished he could wake up and start the day over. All morning he'd been on the phone, begging for more time to pay back his dad's debt. Two lousy extra weeks they'd granted him. Twenty thousand dollars in four weeks. An impossible task.

And now he was being confronted by a woman he'd left naked in a hotel room after impersonating her pen name and dream lover. A woman he craved so much his insides ached, but had no idea how to go about getting. Especially considering that she was standing in front of him, spitting mad, looking for all the world like she believed he was the lowest of the low.

All in all, it was shaping into one hell of an afternoon.

"Well," she persisted, looking particularly cute the way she glared at him with her hands perched on her hips. "Aren't you going to throw some new line my way?"

The urge to laugh almost overwhelmed him. Here he'd taken the chivalrous path, leaving her room before he could actually go through with the scam that would solve all of his financial problems, and to what end? The object of his fascination, the only woman he'd ever desired so tangibly, was standing in his pub, yelling at him, and thinking that he was a no-good, lousy, two-bit con artist.

Well, aren't you?

"Paris, you don't understand—" He stopped himself. The trouble was that she *did* understand. He was his father's son. He was his neighborhood. He was his upbringing. Everything she was accusing him of. Everything he'd been running from his entire life. *You can run, but you can't hide.*

"Don't I? You seem to have mistaken me for one of the characters in my novels. The girls who like to mix it up with the bad guys."

Devin took a breath and came to a decision. *Damn his father, damn the mob and damn himself. He was better than that. She needed to know he was better than that.* "I didn't go through with it. I walked away without going through with it."

Her eyes widened, and she took a tiny step backward. Devin didn't know what she'd expected him to say, but obviously not that. He watched her face as she regrouped.

"So?"

He almost chuckled in relief. That was hardly the fighting response he'd expected. Still, there was an edge to her voice. He wasn't out of the woods yet.

"I didn't blackmail you."

"But you intended to. All those questions about who knows the truth. That wasn't flirting. It wasn't getting-to-know-you talk. You just wanted to use me, and all that talk was nothing but digging and planning to cover your weasely little tracks." She crossed her arms over her chest and tilted her head, her gaze fixed on his eyes. "Well?"

Devin looked at Jerry, then Rachel. Both were entranced, their expressions no help to him. A lie had sucked him into this mess. He'd gamble and try the truth. He noticed the irony and held back a grin.

"Yes," he said simply.

"But you didn't go through with it."

"No."

"Why not?"

Devin paused. Moment of truth time.

"Devin, why?" Paris pressed.

His breath caught in his throat as she spoke his name for the first time. For some idiotic reason, the fact that she'd used his name made him believe they could work everything out. It was a romantic, foolish, sappy notion, but he intended to hold on tight to it anyway.

He nodded toward Jerry, who took the hint. Rachel stayed firmly planted until Paris mouthed the word "go." Then she stood regally and crossed the room, apparently becoming transfixed by the jukebox.

"Why?" Paris repeated, her voice soft. The same voice that had begged him to kiss her. God, this was killing him.

"Because it was you. I couldn't do that. Not to you." He wanted to tell her more, to explain that he'd fallen for her. Hard. But in her mind, she'd just now been introduced to Devin O'Malley. He needed to move slowly and not risk scaring her away.

Her brow furrowed, and her hand went automatically to a strand of hair. When a smile played at the corner of her mouth, he exhaled in relief, only then realizing he'd neglected breathing. It was going to be okay. They would make amends and get to know each other as Devin and Paris. Not Paris and Alexander.

But then she tilted her head and studied the floor. When she looked back up at him, the smile was gone. Her eyes were still warm, but her face was composed. A poker dealer, maybe. Or a lawyer. But not his lover.

"Maybe all your planning wasn't entirely wasted," she said.

"What?" She'd lost him.

"You said you crammed, right?"

He nodded, still not sure where she was going with this.

"And you do seem to have a knack," she added, almost under her breath.

Curiosity battled with irritation. Curiosity won. "A knack for what?" Devin asked.

She shrugged. "Blackmail, gambling. All this intrigue. I understand it runs in the family. And it's so very...Alexanderish."

Devin bristled. Alexander was creeping closer and closer, and Devin was getting pushed out of the picture, replaced by a con artist with a knack for role-playing. That wasn't the Devin he wanted her to see. He wanted her to see the man he'd become—honest, respectable— and he opened his mouth to tell her so.

"Two thousand a week," she said, and Devin closed his mouth.

He swallowed. "Excuse me?"

"The publisher wants to send Alexander on a three-week book tour. Starting tomorrow."

"Tomorrow?"

"The media is clamoring for interviews, and Cobalt Blue wants to strike while the iron is hot. So I need an Alexander. And you owe me." She smiled at him, a real smile with warmth and promise.

She was sexy when she smiled. Devin considered pulling her into his embrace and kissing her the way she'd kissed him in the bar the night before. *That* would get her attention.

Unfortunately, it would also make her point. Planting uninvited kisses on angry women would be like waltzing into Alexander-dom. But if he was with her for three entire weeks, it would be a heck of a lot easier to convince her of his real charms over Alexander's imaginary ones.

He tried to think fast. Jerry could run the pub, and would probably be thrilled to do it just for the extra cash. Jerry might be gruff, but he knew the business. That left the problem of the rest of the money. How the hell could he raise fourteen thousand dollars in the one week left after her tour?

No, he needed time to get the cash he owed. Trouble was, he also needed her. Spending some time with her in close quarters was just the ticket. But three weeks was too much. "If I owe you, I should do it for free. But just one week. No pay."

"Oh, no. I'm not sure what's going on here, but one thing I am sure of is that I don't want to feel obligated to you. Three weeks and you get a paycheck." No smile this time. Just a firm jaw, arms crossed, one hip slightly cocked, as if she was dug in for the duration.

She was sexy when she was stubborn.

He did some fast multiplication. Six thousand from the book tour, another five thousand he could skim from the pub if he scrimped. Two grand he could take off a credit card. That still left him a chunk shy of his goal.

"Make it four a week and you've got a deal."

"I don't think so."

He held up his hands. "I need more."

"I can't afford more. And I doubt I'd pay it if I could. Besides, you got me into this mess, remember?"

That he had. And if he could spare three weeks he'd help her in a heartbeat. He'd just have to compromise.

"How about I do only one week for two grand?" If she agreed, he could scramble to raise the rest of the money in the weeks after the tour. Maybe he could get the earnest money back that he'd put down to buy his second pub in Boston.

And he could always go crawling to Derek as a last resort. He didn't want to, but if that's what it took to help Paris out, he'd suck it up. Somehow, he'd get the money.

"Two weeks."

"One and a half. That's my final offer."

Paris looked toward Rachel, who shrugged.

"We'll make it work somehow," Rachel said.

"Do you think they'll still honor the contract?" Paris asked, and Devin wondered what contract she was worried about.

Rachel shook her head. "I don't know. But we don't have much of a choice, do we?" She shot Devin a withering look.

He held up his hands in surrender. "I can only do a week and a half. I'm sorry. Really."

More sorry than she knew. The possibility of three weeks alone with Paris enticed him, and not only because he wanted time for her to get to know the real Devin. On top of that, he wanted to help her. But it just wasn't possible. If he helped her, he'd never be able to raise the money in time.

Paris nodded. "It's okay. Don't worry. We'll work it out." She held out her hand. "Really. Let's shake on it."

Her handshake was crisp and firm. Businesslike. "You're doing us a huge favor. Really. Thank you," she said.

Devin nodded. "You're welcome."

He felt like a total heel.

6

ONE BY ONE, Paris opened each dresser drawer, making sure nothing was left but plastic hotel laundry bags, the complimentary magazine raving about Manhattan's hot spots, and the Gideon Bible. She moved on to the nightstand and checked its drawer as well. Also empty, except for the room service menu. "I think that's everything except for the closet and a couple of things from the bathroom."

Rachel looked up from her magazine. "I should hope so. You've checked each drawer at least twelve times."

"Only twice." Actually, three times. But Paris doubted Rachel had noticed.

"Three times. I counted. And you don't even leave until tomorrow. Why the big production tonight?"

"I just don't want to forget anything," Paris said, latching on to the first half-truth that flitted through her mind. The real truth was that she wanted to stay busy, needed to keep her mind off Devin. Plus, they'd agreed that he'd spend the night in her connecting room so that she could coach him this evening, and so they could ride together to the airport in the morning.

With Devin just a thin wall away, Paris doubted she'd be able to concentrate on packing if she waited until morning.

Rachel stood up and crossed to the bed, peering down

at the stacks of clothes and bags of cosmetics. "I already see something you've forgotten."

"Really?" Paris inventoried her belongings, comparing the list in her head to the piles on the bed. "What?"

Rachel squatted on the floor and rummaged in her leather tote bag, then pitched a handful of condoms into Paris's open suitcase. "I've only got a half dozen here. But between you, me and the hotel furniture, I haven't really needed them lately. There's a shortage of good men in this city. And since you just snagged the last one, you'll need to pick up a pack at the airport tomorrow morning."

Paris glanced at the neon packets shining like Mardi Gras coins, then up at Rachel, who was doing a poor job of holding back a grin. *With friends like this…*

"First, I am not going to sleep with him. And second, even if I were, I would not in a million years suggest a lime green fluorescent condom."

"The hot pink is nice."

"Third," Paris continued, ignoring her once-best friend who had just slipped below Paris's goldfish on the friendship scale. She stopped, confused. "I know I had a third."

"Third, you're going to be a martyr for women everywhere and turn down the attention of this amazing looking guy who is obviously crazy about you."

"Yes," said Paris. "I mean, no. I am not being a martyr."

"You were going to do the deed last night."

"Last night I didn't know that he almost *blackmailed* me. This is not a good start for a relationship. Dr. Laura would not approve."

"But he didn't blackmail you. He's honorable. Chivalrous. Oozing with character."

"Just because he walked away from one blackmail scheme doesn't make him Sir Lancelot. Knights in shining armor don't think up clever ways to use women to get money. Besides, maybe he walked away because my dad's a judge and not because his chivalrous side overwhelmed him."

Or maybe he does like you. She squashed the thought, then grabbed a pair of khakis from the closet and started folding them on the bed. What was the world coming to when she was arguing with her best friend *and* herself?

Rachel stood sideways in front of the mirror mounted on the closet door, stomach sucked in, chest out. She turned and checked her other side.

Paris watched, amused. "What are you doing?"

"Sagging. No wonder he's smitten with you. You don't sag."

"Rach, gravity doesn't even know where you live. And he's not smitten with me."

Rachel dropped the pose. "Oh, I know smitten. And he is it."

"It was a one-night thing, set in motion because he wanted to get something from me. Even if he did walk away from his little racket, that doesn't mean he's smitten."

She concentrated on folding her clothes, warding off erotic memories of the night before. Her thoughts had no business going there. No matter how much she'd melted from his touch, she was not about to fall under the spell of some con artist who intended to use her just to make a buck. And for a gambling debt! Maybe if he'd needed the money to buy a kidney for his grandmother…

She shook the thought away. Her imagination might be able to come up with noble reasons for his scheme, but that didn't make them true.

"Everything is on an even keel now. It's a business arrangement, pure and simple. That's all. No repeats of last night. I need an Alexander, and he fits the bill." Her body regretted the decision, but her head knew it was for the best.

"So now you're the one using him."

Paris considered. "Yeah. I guess I am. Well, good for me. After all, turnabout's fair play. And at least I hired him."

"Oh, I'm not criticizing," said Rachel, flopping on the bed. "In fact, that makes it even better."

Paris almost cringed at the devious tone in Rachel's voice. "Better how?"

"If it's a business arrangement, he can still be your boy toy. It's so yuppie. One and a half weeks. That's the perfect length for a fling. A little diversion, take your mind off work. And you're hitting California and Vegas. How decadent is that?"

The laugh escaped before Paris could stop it. *Great, now Rachel would be encouraged.* She put on a stern face. "Decadent is not the image we're going for here. I don't need a boy toy or your advice." She waved her arm around the room. "All of this is the result of you shooting off your mouth at the bar that night."

"The room?"

"The situation, dummy," Paris said, lobbing a pillow at her intentionally dense friend. "I don't need any more complications in my life. Certainly not a complication with a gambling debt the size of Alaska. I can't get involved with some scheming, gambling, street-savvy con artist."

Paris held up a hand against Rachel's inevitable comment. "And I realize he did't go through with it, but that's not the point. I don't do flings well. It would be just my luck that I'd fall for him, and then where would I be?"

Of course, the better question was, *How did she un-fall for him?* The damage was already done, but Paris wasn't going to admit that to Rachel. The way out of this mess was to just take it one step at a time, and to keep the relationship purely professional. Any hints of sexual tension, and she'd politely turn the conversation back to their work.

Then she'd take a cold shower.

"Okay, you win," said Rachel. "Have a nice boring little tour. Maybe you'll meet a valet in Vegas who'll sweep you off your feet."

"Thank you," said Paris, grateful to steer away from the dangerous direction her thoughts were headed.

There would be nothing smart about getting mixed up with a fantasy man, and Paris was not a stupid girl.

"HERE I AM. Putty in your hands." Devin leaned negligently against the door frame, a canvas duffel bag slung over one shoulder, his tattered navy T-shirt just tight enough to show there was nothing soft or malleable about this man. He was hard. Stone. As immovable as a mountain.

"Hi. Come on in." Paris stepped aside to let the mountain enter.

Rachel would consider this a personal challenge. *He wants to be putty*, she'd say. *By the time I'm done he'll be mush.* But Rachel had the seductress act down cold, not Paris. Even if Paris could, what would be the point? A week of savage, wild sex, and then what?

Isn't that enough? Paris imagined Rachel's amazed query.

Paris ignored her friend's urging, as well as her own hesitant agreement. No matter how alluring he might be, she'd squashed all intentions of picking up where they'd left off. He'd been setting her up for blackmail, after all. Best she kept that little fact firmly in mind.

She shut the door and turned around. He waited a few

feet behind her, just on the threshold of the main area of the hotel room. Despite her self-imposed mini-lecture, the desire to reach out and stroke his chest almost overwhelmed her.

Damn Rachel. She was such a bad influence.

How was she going to manage such close quarters with this gorgeous hunk of tanned, muscular, blond...*maleness* if she couldn't control her eyes, much less her hands?

She tried to manage a businesslike smile. He watched her, a quizzical expression playing across his features. "What is it?" she asked, fearing he could read her mind.

"Three weeks."

"What?"

"You heard me. I'm yours for three weeks. I got you into this, the least I can do is help you get out." His jaw was firm. Was he expecting her to argue?

"I can only afford to pay you two a week."

He nodded. "I know."

"But...I thought you needed—"

"Do you want me for three weeks or not?"

"Of course," she answered, ignoring the devilish voice in her head that urged her to blurt out the kind of thoughts his words inspired. "I just don't want to mess things up for you."

How pitiful is that? Paris wondered. Suddenly the last thing she wanted to do was inconvenience him. *What's wrong with this picture?*

Devin's smile softened his entire face. "Thanks. I appreciate that. But I'll be fine. Really."

"What changed your mind?"

"Some obligations I'm just not willing to turn my back on."

"Oh," she blurted. "A code. Like honor among thieves."

She regretted the words the second they left her tongue, even before she saw him wince. "Oh, gosh. I'm sorry," she said uselessly. He was at least making an effort at chivalry and she was insulting him.

He waved a hand and gave her the slightest of nods. "So, we're leaving in the morning?" he asked.

Paris considered whether to apologize again. Probably better to drop it. "Yeah. Bright and early."

"Well, then, what's on the agenda tonight?" Nothing in his tone suggested he was thinking about a repeat of the night before. Didn't matter, Paris thought about it anyway.

"Training." She smiled sweetly, forcing her mind back on track. "Brutal, hard-core basic training. If you're going into battle for me, I want you prepared." Her eyes grazed his body again and she choked back a sigh. The real battle was raging in her. She'd managed to keep her hands in check for all of four minutes. That deserved a pat on the back.

He dropped his shoulder and let his bag slide to the floor. "Fair enough. Where do we start?"

"Ground rules," Paris said, with force intended more for herself than him. "We need to establish the basic ground rules."

"Great. Shoot."

Paris frowned. Something was wrong, but she couldn't put her finger on it.

"So what's our first ground rule?" he pressed.

"You're Devin," she said, ignoring his question as she realized what was troubling her.

"Hate to break it to you, but your rule doesn't make sense."

"No. I mean, yes. No. I mean you *are* Devin."

"Yes. Me, Devin. You, Paris."

Paris ignored his sarcasm. "I mean your hair is blond. That's not Alexander." Her stomach turned as she considered the uncomfortable truth. This blond-haired devil— not Alexander—had swept her off her feet.

His con, remember? He pretended to be Alexander to get you in bed. To get your money. And he did a damn good job.

She felt like bopping herself on the forehead. Of course! Certainly she hadn't fallen for this man. No way. Just for his Alexander-ness.

Well, she wasn't about to make the same mistake twice.

A muscle twitched in his cheek and he took a few breaths before speaking. "Sorry. I didn't realize I needed to be good old Monty every waking minute. Since I'm not trying to pull anything over on you, I thought I'd just be myself for now." His eyes held a challenge, but Paris didn't understand the contest.

"I'm hiring you because I need an Alexander on this tour. If someone figures out you're not really Alexander, then I'm in a lot of trouble."

"You mean someone like me?" A hard edge laced his voice.

He seemed defensive, and her guard went up, parrying his thrusts with sarcasm. "You think I'm worried about unscrupulous scoundrels learning my secret and blackmailing me? No. I figure that's probably a once-in-a-lifetime kind of thing."

Paris thought she saw hurt flash in his eyes, but it was gone before she could be sure.

She took a breath. "Look, that's not what bothers me. I realize it may be a pain, but the fact is that Alexander's never been on tour before. No one's ever *seen* him before, at least not until the party. What if someone sneaks into the room? Follows us? Peers in a window? At the very least, you need to always look Alexanderish, even if you talk Devin. Don't you see? I can't risk the truth. I need this contract."

Some of the tenseness seemed to melt from him. "Fair enough. I guess we start with hair dye." He leaned over and rummaged around in his battered canvas bag, eventually pulling out a box. He held it out to her. "Bold and Brilliant Chestnut. Got it on sale. Permanent this time. Want to do the honors?"

SHE SHOULD HAVE SAID NO, Paris realized later, as she ran her fingers through his damp hair, massaging in the conditioner that had come in the package. Without thinking, she'd walked smack into a predicament designed to test her resolve.

Devin balanced on the edge of the bathtub, bare feet inside, his tan shoulders and sinewy back naked except for the small, white towel draped over him. At least his legs were covered by the ratty blue sweatpants he'd changed into before they'd started this whole hair thing. The last thing Paris needed was the distraction of seeing his well-muscled thighs extending under a pair of shorts or straining against tight denim.

From behind him, Paris couldn't see his chest, but she remembered the smattering of hair that matched the still-golden locks gliding over her fingers. His hair seemed silkier tonight, probably because he'd washed out the color. Her fingertips recalled the coarse strands she'd stroked the night before.

Had it only been one night?

Paris remembered the pleasure of his hands on her skin, touching and stroking. His kisses, hot and wild. She barely realized that her fingers were grasping tighter, pulling his head back. He followed with his body, leaning against her until his bare back pressed against her stomach, and his head rested against her breasts. She could see the rise and fall of his chest as he breathed. Closing her eyes, she could feel the rhythm of her own heartbeat, its tempo increasing, pounding.

"Paris." Devin's voice was low, almost inaudible, but the way he said her name cut straight to her core. "I think you're supposed to add the gel sometime before my hair dries."

With a start, she opened her eyes. "Oh. I...um...I was just thinking." Biting back a curse, she scolded herself for getting sidetracked so easily.

"You're supposed to pull your own hair out when you think. Not someone else's."

She looked down and saw her fingers knotted in his hair. "Sorry. I was—"

"—thinking. I know." He twisted at the waist until she could see his face. "What were you thinking about?" His cockeyed grin suggested he had some idea already.

A little white lie flew to her lips. "The publicity tour. Details. You know." That was half-true, after all.

"Really."

Why did she get the feeling he didn't believe her? She stepped back, and her hands automatically went to her hips, as she adopted her little-used, I'm-in-control-here courtroom stance. *Your Honor, just because my client has millions socked away in the Caymans doesn't mean he embezzled it. Yeah, right.*

She forced a smile. "Yes, really. I've been thinking about a lot of things. Planning, you know? Stuff to do." She waved nonchalantly in his direction, as if he was just one of a dozen tasks awaiting her. "We have to rehearse you, for example."

"Uh-huh."

"You don't believe me?" She immediately regretted the

question. *Of course* he didn't believe her. And he was right. Not that it mattered. Thinking and doing were two entirely different things.

His smile started slow, but soon dominated his face. "Oh, I believe you."

"You do?" Paris stared at him, amazed she'd pulled off *that* coup.

"Sure. I believe you were thinking about your ground rules." The smile changed, losing some innocence, gaining some seductive appeal, and becoming ever-so-much-more interesting in the process.

Interesting and kissable.

Paris yanked the thought away. "Right. Ground rules."

"I was doing a little thinking about rules myself." He pointed at the small plastic bottle sitting on the edge of the bathtub. "If you're finished conditioning, maybe you should rub that in now."

"Sure. Before your hair dries." His shift in topic had distracted her, and she was left wondering what rules he had come up with. She snipped the tip of the bottle off with nail scissors, then slipped on the flimsy plastic gloves that had come in the package. "Turn around," she ordered.

His back to her again, she frowned, unable to shake the feeling that he was toying with her. She massaged the gel through his hair, pulled off the gloves and set the alarm on her watch for fifteen minutes.

Not a word from Devin. He still hadn't clued her in on his rules.

Paris cleared her throat and spoke to the back of his neck. "So, what is it you were thinking about? Rules, I mean." She hoped her voice came out casual. At least it hadn't cracked.

Silence. Then he bent forward and turned on the tap,

running his wrist under the water and fiddling with the controls until the temperature was right. Only then did he turn his head and look back at her over his extended arm.

His eyes beckoned, and her body warmed in response.

"There's an attraction between us." He straightened up and stood as he spoke, crossing the small space in one step, ending up so close that she could feel his breath on her face.

She opened her mouth to deny it, but no words came out.

"Don't you think so?" he added.

Paris squared her shoulders. They needed to be talking rules. Business. Now was not the time for her insides to get mushy.

He tucked a stray strand of hair behind her ear. The erotic caress made her dizzy.

"Paris? The least you can do is admit the attraction. We were both there, remember?"

She nodded, poise and composure slipping away. "Of course. Yes. Yes, there's an attraction. Sure."

One breath. Then another. And another.

Okay, maybe this wasn't so bad, where the conversation was going. This was good. Talking about this attraction, desire, lust, whatever. It was necessary. Her whole purpose was to lay their major ground rule. No repeats of last night. Nothing but work. So he'd led the conversation in totally the right direction. She just needed to tell him.

She cleared her throat. "Devin, I—"

"We'll have to fight it. We shouldn't let anything more happen." He stroked her cheek, a friendly gesture that left a trail of fire. "You know. Professional distance. I think that would be best."

"That's really what you think?" They were all words she had planned to say. So why was she so disappointed?

"Of course," Devin continued, his voice low. "Although I can see your point, too. You may be right. Yes, you just might be absolutely right on this one."

"I might?" *Her point? Did she have a point?* What kind of game was he playing?

He nodded. "It's difficult to tell which is the better route."

Paris opened her mouth to ask what he was talking about, but her wristwatch alarm beeped, stalling the question. Thank goodness. She needed a moment to get her head together. This wasn't going at all like she'd planned.

She plastered on a professional smile. "Rinse time," she sang. "Do you want to just pop into the shower?"

He perched on the edge of the tub again, and slowly shook his head. This time his feet were on the outside, and Paris had a feeling she knew what was coming.

"It's just as easy for you to do it." As he spoke, he grabbed her hips, urging her forward, and Paris vaguely wondered if his fingers would singe her. "I'll just tilt my head backward," he added as he gently positioned her over him.

As she straddled him, one leg on either side of his knees, Devin passed her a cup filled with water. Paris forced herself to concentrate. She poured the water over his head, and it flowed down his hair and into the tub. They repeated the exercise, waiting for the water to flow clear instead of inky.

The intimacy of the position was undeniable. So was the danger, Paris realized, as she let another stream of water trickle over him. Not that she feared falling. The danger lurked in the heat they were generating, in the way Paris was aware of the spot inside her thigh just above her knee that kept rubbing against his leg.

Once again she reminded herself. Thinking. Doing.

Two entirely different things. And *doing* was not on the agenda.

He passed her another cupful of water. But instead of retreating to the edge of the tub as before, his hand lightly gripped the back of her leg, his finger idly stroking.

Fighting her body's response, Paris grabbed a dry towel from the rack and ran it over his head, working the water out until nothing was left but damp curls.

As soon as she removed the towel, she sucked in her breath. Moments before, his appeal had been undeniable. But now he was larger than life. He was Alexander, a man straight from her fantasies. Straight from between her sheets on nights when she couldn't sleep and lay awake dreaming, wondering, hoping that someday he'd step into her life.

She shook herself. Alexander wasn't real, and it was Devin in her bathroom, half-naked and tempting her.

She realized what he was up to. He had said she was right, but he knew perfectly well she had no idea what she was supposedly right about. He wanted her to ask.

Paris didn't want to play his game, didn't want to lose control of the situation. But she really did want to know. *And, girlfriend, you are already way out of control.* Besides, the torment of his finger drawing lazy patterns on the back of her leg was going to drive her mad.

Round one, Mr. O'Malley.

"Okay, what might I be right about?"

"Intimacy." His eyes didn't open.

"Excuse me?"

"Intimacy. Appearances. Comfort zone." He opened his eyes and they held no challenge. Just desire. Paris took a step backward, but his hand tightened around the back of her calf. He straightened his head, and Paris realized with mortification that he was eye level with her breasts.

And she was wearing a T-shirt. With no bra. In a humid bathroom. So much for playing it cool.

"I don't know what you mean," Paris said truthfully, hoping she didn't sound rattled.

"There's an intimacy between you and Alexander. An understanding. You're supposed to know each other so well. If we're fighting this...thing...between us, there'll be tension, nerves. People will be able to tell." His hand slid up the back of her leg, his fingers boldly caressing her inner thigh, until finally cupping the curve of her rear.

Paris was pretty sure her kneecaps were melting.

"If there's an intimacy between us, people will realize," he went on. "They won't know what kind, of course, but they'll recognize the closeness and your scam won't be in jeopardy."

"Is that..." her voice sounded husky. She cleared her throat, conjuring her normal speaking voice, determined to fight against what was happening to her body. And to her head. "Is that the way to pull a scam?"

"Trust me on this one." He leaned forward, urging her toward him with his hand even as he leaned forward from the waist. His mouth closed over her breast before Paris could think, and then all she could do was react. Her nipple hardened under the attack of his tongue through the thin material. Her legs turned to rubber as warm honey flowed through her body. She had to sit before she fell, and she sank to the floor. His mouth and hand released her, and she ended up perched at his feet while he smiled down at her, warm and inviting and, oh, so tempting.

Thinking. Not doing. Her new mantra.

"And I thought through all of that, huh?" she asked, when her voice worked again.

He nodded. "Oh, yeah. A brilliant piece of reasoning,

actually." He leaned over and plugged the tub, readjusting the temperature on the still-running tap. Then he uncapped a bottle of hotel-supplied bubble bath and poured it into the stream.

"Three weeks, right?" He held out a hand to her and helped her up from the floor.

"Right. So?"

Devin put one leg over the side of the tub and stepped in. Paris leaned over for a closer look. A thin layer of bubbly water covered the bottom of the oversized tub. She looked back at him, eyebrows raised.

Then he swung the other foot over, sat down, and stretched out in the tub, sweatpants and all.

"Devin!"

"What?" He looked genuinely shocked at her outburst. "Three weeks isn't very long. I figure we've got no time to waste getting started on that intimacy idea of yours."

"But, but..." She had no clue what to say. "Your pants."

He shrugged, the picture of indifference. "Oh, don't worry. They'll drip-dry."

Paris knew her mouth was hanging open. She felt like the only one in the room who didn't get the joke, and she was positive there *was* a joke.

He pulled his legs up, freeing half the bathtub. Then he splashed the water as if he were patting a seat cushion. "Aren't you coming in?"

The evening was getting weirder and weirder. Paris searched her mind, trying to figure out some way to articulate the utter bizarreness of the situation.

"What?" she finally sputtered. It was the best she could come up with.

Devin nodded sagely. "No, you're right. Once again, you have a point." A wide grin lit up his face, and his eyes sparkled with mischief. "You're batting a thousand tonight."

As if she'd stepped into a cartoon, a lightbulb turned on over Paris's head. This time he was going to say that she was right about their intimacy. How could they really be close if they were wearing clothes?

She imagined him loosening the drawstring of his pants, raising his hips up and letting the waterlogged pants slide off his well-muscled legs. She pictured the way he would look, sitting there in the tub, water beading on his skin. His smile when he held out a hand to her, urging her forward. The heat from his fingers as he loosened her own pants and then grazed her hips as he slid the material down to the tile floor. Her body warmed as she imagined his eyes taking her in before she joined him in the warm, scented water.

She sighed. A nice fantasy, but it wasn't going to happen.

"I'm sorry," she said to the floor. She looked up and saw disappointment flash in his eyes. And something else. Determination, maybe? "It's an interesting suggestion, but I think we'll stick with the no-intimacy version of the rules."

Devin nodded. "I understand."

"Are you mad?"

There was no mistaking his surprise. "That you said no? Of course not."

"That I didn't stop you before you drenched your pants."

"Nah, they needed washing anyway. I'll just hang out here and give them a good soaking."

Paris laughed. "We'll jump right into the Alexander lessons tomorrow." She nodded at the tub. "That was not an Alexander-like thing to do."

No, not at all. But very endearing nonetheless.

"Lessons are fine. Just don't forget that I'm not Alexander. I'm Devin. All of me." He crossed his arms behind his back and stretched, his chest muscles rippling.

She cleared her throat, the now-familiar fluster returning. "Yes, well, stay as long as you want. You can have this room and I'll sleep in the connecting one."

She turned to leave, then paused, turning back to him. "Devin?"

His eyes were closed. "Hmm?"

"You never had any intention of following ground rules, did you?"

"*'I'd gladly sidestep any rule if it keeps me from my mission.'*" He opened his eyes. "*'Or from another taste of you.'*"

She drew a shaky breath. Another line from her first book. He was Alexander, and yet he wasn't. Her dream lover, and at the same time a flesh and blood man—fascinating and sexy. And dangerous.

She steeled herself, then nodded at Devin, fearing that any attempt to talk would end her up in his arms. She slid out of the bathroom and pulled the door shut behind her.

Memories of his caresses, his scent, his charm drifted through her mind. She sighed. It would be a long night.

But at least she'd won Round Two.

7

"HALF-NAKED IN A BATHTUB? And you left? Are you ill?" Rachel extended a hand to feel Paris's forehead.

"Will you stop?" Paris swatted Rachel's hand away, glancing around the busy LaGuardia airport gift shop.

A well-tanned older couple wearing matching Bermuda shorts and clashing Hawaiian print shirts glanced her way. Paris smiled politely, hoping they were staring because they were nosy, and not because they'd overheard Rachel's comments.

Then again, maybe they were looking at the dark circles she was sure lined the undersides of her eyes. She hadn't slept at all last night, too distracted by the man in the next room. But now victory was hers, and Rachel wasn't going to spoil it. Especially considering how hard-fought the battle had been. "I told you I wasn't going to sleep with him. And I meant it."

"Well, goodie for you. You win the jackpot. Biff the Wonder Accountant, a thrill-a-minute life playing hostess at Daddy's and hubby's parades of political functions, a nanny and a prescription for Prozac. How excited you must be."

"Rachel." Paris shot her a warning look.

Rachel threw her hands up in surrender. "Hey, not that there's anything wrong with that. If that's what you want." Rachel slapped a magazine and a packet of gum down on the counter. "But I think you're just avoiding the truth."

Paris rolled her eyes. "I wouldn't have even told you if I'd known you'd go psychoanalyst on me. In fact, I wouldn't have had you drive us. Devin and I would have just taken a taxi."

Rachel shrugged and paid the clerk, a dark-haired girl who looked about sixteen. "It's not too late to stock up on those condoms. You still might need them."

The clerk giggled. Paris aimed a dirty look at Rachel, then added a candy bar to her own stack of paperback novels. "What magazine did Devin say to get him?"

"Um," Rachel scanned the magazine rack and pointed to a dense weekly finance and investment report. "Guess our little scrapper's into light reading, huh?" She nudged Paris. "Maybe you can mold him into your accountant."

Paris gave her a level stare. "Just pass me the magazine."

She paid the girl, who Paris was sure was holding back a smirk. On the way to the gate, Rachel coughed once. Then again. Paris looked at her.

"Nothing," Rachel said, all innocence.

"I'm not sleeping with him," she said, her gaze automatically drifting toward the bank of pay phones halfway down the concourse where Devin stood, the receiver pressed to his ear.

"Right. I know. You've made that perfectly clear."

Paris stopped dead, almost tripping a woman struggling with a massive suitcase. "Why are you making it your personal project to attach me to this guy? You're practically begging me to sleep with him. And despite all your talk, that's not your normal routine. So why are you pushing it on me? Do you win a prize or something if you manage to compromise my virtue?"

"Not me. You win the prize. A lifetime membership in the Club of Lost Virtue. Or..." She took a step back, arms crossed over her chest, and scanned Paris from head to foot.

"Or, what?"

"Maybe he's The One. You'll fall madly in love, and your virtues can ride off into the sunset together."

Paris laughed. "Since when did you become the romantic type?"

"I liked *Sleepless in Seattle*. I cried during *Titanic*."

"Only because she dropped the necklace in the Atlantic."

"Even so. Mark my words. I have a feeling he might be it."

Paris frowned. Rachel needed to hurry up and get over this Paris-Devin kick before she resorted to something rash. Paris pictured Devin handcuffed to her in a locked candlelit room, and Rachel not letting them out until they finally did the deed.

Of course, that might not be such a bad thing. Paris pictured Devin laid out on the bed, his arms stretched wide and kept firmly in place by silk ribbons. No, by Paris's black silk stockings. Chest bare, she could tease and torment him with her kisses until his skin danced with passion and he writhed beneath her at only a whisper of her touch.

Paris sighed and opened her eyes. This was not the place to be thinking those kinds of thoughts. No, she corrected, she shouldn't be thinking those thoughts *anywhere*. Plan, remember? Right kind of man, remember?

But thirty minutes later, as she sat tucked into her cramped little airplane seat, Rachel's prediction still rang in her mind.

The One? Not possible. Paris was a sensible girl, and

sensible girls did not fall madly in love with con artists. A smile touched her lips. Not even ones that read the financial pages, spoke eloquently about kisses and thought up goofy plans that involved taking a bath fully clothed? No, she told herself sternly, not even those.

But do sensible girls write thrill-a-minute spy novels with half-naked femme fatales lurking in the hero's bed?

With a yank, she cinched the seat belt tighter. *This* girl did. She wrote novels, she fantasized about her invented author and she hired a mystery man to impersonate her pen name. But even if he was a complete hunk, and even if she was attracted to him, and even if her hormones were working overtime, she wasn't going to fall for him.

Not hard anyway.

She was going to stick to her plan and get her life back on track so that she could tell her dad what she did for a living and marry some nice, normal guy and live happily ever after.

Paris shot an irritated look toward Devin, buried in one of her books. She scowled. He didn't even have a clue about her angst. *Men.*

She gave the restraint one more tug for good measure and made sure her seat and tray table were in the full upright and locked position. When the attendant held up an emergency procedures card, Paris scrambled in the pocket to find hers.

Devin wasn't even paying attention. He seemed engrossed in Alexander's third book. The plane could go down in flames and he'd have no clue about which exit to head for.

She looked up to find the oxygen masks that would fall in an emergency. The ceiling seemed pretty solid. What if her mask was in there too tight?

She turned to Devin, but he didn't seem interested, and

his nonchalance fanned her already sparked irritation. She took a breath and tried to think of that mantra. Something about lotus flowers. Okay. Everything was okay. If the plane crashed Paris could take care of herself.

Oh, Lord, surely it wouldn't crash.

Devin turned a page, glancing up slightly, and caught her eye. A smile tugged at his mouth. His kissable mouth.

Paris frowned and dropped her eyes, concentrating on the emergency card in her lap. Rachel was just flat wrong. That was all there was to it. He surely wasn't the one. He was all wrong. Nothing like Paris had planned for. Nothing like what her father expected or would approve of.

She had her entire life and career to think about. Family expectations. Appearances. She'd be silly to sabotage all that by giving in to a couple of weeks of passion. Even really, really intense passion.

She jumped a mile at the gentle nudge on her shoulder.

"Sorry." His brow furrowed. "Are you all right?"

"Sure. Yes. Of course." She peered at him. "Why are you asking? Don't I look all right?"

He nodded toward her lap. Paris followed his gaze and winced. She'd managed to inflict serious damage on the emergency card. Bent corners, little tears, creases and crinkles.

"My mind wanders," she said.

"I can see that."

"And I don't much like flying."

"No kidding."

It was like sitting next to a tub of dynamite. Paris didn't know what to do, what to say. She wanted to explore this thing, this desire, that crackled between them, even as she wanted to run screaming from it.

The silence thickened.

Getting any work done with him was going to be murder, and she still had four hours on this plane with him before they landed in Los Angeles. Not to mention over five hundred hours on the ground. Traveling together. Working together. Closely. *Intimately.*

The hum of the engines increased and Paris felt the pressure of acceleration push her back in the seat. Her fingers tightened around the armrest and she closed her eyes.

The surprise of his palm on the back of her hand took her mind away from the takeoff. His caress was gentle, but still firm and reassuring. Paris opened her eyes and smiled a silent thank-you as the plane lifted into the air. He squeezed her hand, and Paris instantly wished he hadn't. Every nerve ending below her wrist was on fire, and each of those nerves had a high-speed connection to the depths of her heart.

The wrong kind of thoughts started wandering through her mind. Images of his shoulders, his thighs, the memory of the elevator and his breath on the back of her neck.

Something about a mile-high club. She shivered.

"Are you going to be okay?"

"What? Oh, the plane. Yeah. It's takeoff that gets me the most. I'm fine. Really." She glanced down at their intertwined hands, then back up quickly before he could notice.

Too late. He let go of her hand. When she looked at him, he seemed sad, but the effect was fleeting.

"You distracted me," she said, walking into dangerous territory. "I guess I should say thanks."

"You're welcome." He sat up straighter and turned to face her. "So, did you sleep okay last night?"

Her response was immediate and honest. "No."

"Me neither," he said, shifting in his seat and relaxing a

little. "It'll be hard getting through three weeks on no sleep."

"Somehow we'll muddle through."

"It's a bummer." The corner of his mouth twitched and Paris knew he was teasing.

"What?"

"'Round the clock employment, but no fringe benefits." He spread his hands, imploring. "What's a poor boy to do?"

Paris grinned and smacked his hand away. He was too quick and caught her fingers, his hand engulfing hers. She gave a gentle tug, but he held on.

"Gotcha." He gave a quick, gentle kiss to her fingertips, sending her mind whirling. "I think I'll just have to keep a tight hold on management until we can negotiate better terms."

No doubt he was thinking about the same type of terms that were running through her mind. Terms that involved more than just touching fingertips.

She mentally waggled a finger at herself. *Ah-ah-ah. Rules, remember? Plans? He's been officially working for you for less than twenty-four hours. Get a grip and control your lust.*

She smiled sweetly. "You're not exactly being paid minimum wage." She pulled her hand free, and as her fingers slid away, the ability to think coherently returned.

She regarded him out of the corner of her eye. He didn't look at all guilty about trying to change her mind. Persistent devil. "Nice try," she allowed.

"Thanks. Did I gain any ground?"

"No." *And if you did, I wouldn't tell you.*

"Oh, well. Too bad. But I had to try."

"Why?"

He tapped his finger against his chin. "Why? Hmm. I'd have to say testosterone, mostly."

"It's amazing how accurate some stereotypes are. Men are just ruled by their—"

"—right. It's true. We're a lowly lot." He pretended to pout.

He was pretty cute when he was being lowly.

"Well, all that aside, we're keeping a safe distance between us. Platonic. Professional," she insisted.

"Safe for whom?"

Paris ignored him.

"Are you sure that's what you want?" he asked.

"Devin. I told you. You distract me."

His eyes found hers, and Paris was sure he could see all her secrets.

"I like to distract you," he whispered, in a voice that zeroed in on her core.

She took a breath. *Steady. Steady.* "We need to work. You're the hired help, remember?"

"I'm gunning for a promotion."

Paris did her best to conjure up a seductive smile worthy of Rachel. "Well, then, you know what they say," she said, lowering her voice to a husky whisper.

He didn't look like he was buying it for a second, but he played along. "What?"

"Performance counts."

"I'll like earning this promotion."

She pulled a three-inch thick binder out of her tote bag and dropped it into his lap. "This. You get to perform this."

"I'm guessing this isn't the *Kama Sutra*," Devin deadpanned.

"You're very astute." She flipped to the first section. "You can start with the plot lines of Alexander's books."

THREE HOURS LATER, Devin closed the notebook, his eyes sore from reading. He hoped he could keep it all straight. The last thing he wanted to do was let her down.

Devin had to give her points for organization. Her notebook certainly made his job a lot easier. Press clippings, time lines, a fifty-page bio of Alexander, complete with birthplace and educational background. It was all there. A complete primer on Montgomery Alexander. The bloody British bastard.

With a sigh, he leaned back in his seat. He'd agreed to play her Monty in public. Like he'd said, it was his performance that created this mess for her. In private, however, he intended to convince her that she wanted him, not some fantasy she'd crafted over the years. He'd play Alexander, sure. But he'd let Devin seep in around the edges. Until finally, in private, there would be only him. Devin.

And when that happened, he didn't want there to be any doubt in her mind about who was holding her and loving her. That was the real reason he'd agreed to this tour. The only reason he'd sucked up his pride and committed to three weeks—even though that meant he'd probably have to crawl to Derek when he got back to New York.

Maybe he'd get lucky. Jerry promised to canvass all their friends from the old neighborhood who'd gone legit. He'd end up indebted to half of New York and most of New Jersey, but it would be worthwhile if he got Paris in the end.

And he had every intention of getting Paris back in his arms and keeping her there.

Old Monty could take a flying leap.

Paris mumbled something in her sleep and shifted her position, the flimsy blue blanket dropping from her shoulder. Devin reached over and tucked it around her, unable to resist the urge to stroke her cheek as he pulled his hand away. She stirred, turning her face toward him and prolonging the contact.

He imagined her in bed, asleep, curling her body against his, instinctively seeking his warmth, his touch. It was a dangerous place for his thoughts to go. His body was already reacting to the image of Paris, naked beside him, her skin and hair glinting in candlelight.

Very dangerous. And very, very appealing.

She moved again in the seat beside him, pulling the blanket tighter around her. He chuckled. She probably hogged the covers. That was okay. A small price to pay.

Devin reached over and brushed a wild curl away from her face.

"Are we there yet?" she mumbled, her voice thick with sleep. He pulled his hand away.

Paris sat up and squinted at him. "Do we land soon?"

"Welcome back. I think we're over California. Probably about a half hour more."

"Devin? Thanks for agreeing to the whole tour. I appreciate it." She dropped her eyes. "And thanks for agreeing to keep it purely professional."

"Well, I'm not so sure I willingly agreed to that." She looked up, alarm shining in her eyes. "But, hey, a deal's a deal. The lady wants it purely professional, then professional it is."

Devin allowed himself a tiny grin. *But that didn't mean he couldn't try to change the lady's mind.*

8

"IT'S AN HONOR having you stay here, Mr. Alexander. Really. An honor. I just love your books." The bellhop stopped the luggage cart in front of the elevator bank of the swank Santa Monica hotel.

"Thank you," Devin said. He gestured to the call button. "It'll come faster if you push the button."

"Oh. Right. I'm just... Wow." The boy jabbed the up-arrow.

Devin squelched a grin, and looked at Paris. She scowled at him and crossed her arms over her chest. Then she examined her watch and looked back up at Devin.

He shrugged, not sure what was annoying her. Maybe the taxi drive. Even after the morning rush hour, Los Angeles freeways weren't exactly a picnic, and although their driver spoke no English, he seemed to have a fascination with rap music played at deafening levels. Paris probably just needed to relax.

The elevator dinged, and the doors slid open. "Right this way, Mr. Alexander." The boy wheeled the luggage cart in, holding the door open just long enough for Devin to enter. Paris jumped in as the doors were sliding shut. She shot the bellhop a dirty look, but Devin doubted the boy noticed since he was so intent on staring at the famous Mr. Montgomery Alexander.

This sudden dive into celebrity was turning out to be a wild ride. He checked to see if Paris shared his amusement. She rewarded him with a look even dirtier than the one she'd laid on the boy. Okay. So she wasn't amused.

She turned her back to him and faced the closed doors. Her arms were crossed in front of her again, her foot tapped a rhythm, and her back was rigid. She looked ready to explode.

She also looked damn sexy.

What was it with the two of them and elevators?

A light, cotton button-down covered every inch of her back and arms, but it didn't matter. In his mind, Devin could still see the glow of her milky-white skin revealed as he coaxed her zipper down. He delighted in remembering her warmth under his fingertips, her fervent response to his touch.

The elevator stopped at the fourteenth floor. Just in time, thought Devin. He needed a shower. A cold one.

The bellhop led them down the narrow hallway. "Okay. Miss, you're right here." He opened Paris's door, then dropped her suitcase inside the threshold. "Enjoy your stay."

Paris rolled her eyes to the ceiling, nodded curtly at Devin, then slammed the door. The bellhop scurried back to the luggage cart. "And Mr. Alexander, you're in the next room here."

"It connects to the lady's room, right?"

"Oh, yes, sir, Mr. Alexander, sir." The boy winked as he left, and Devin was glad Paris wasn't around to notice.

The room was simple, but comfortable. Devin eyed the double bed right away, along with the closed door to Paris's room. He crossed to it and rapped lightly. "Paris?"

"Not now."

Devin resisted the urge to use the key the bellhop had given him. She'd been fine when they'd left the airport, but now she was as cold as ice. Surely she wasn't ticked off because one of the hotel staff lacked basic manners.

He knocked again.

"I'm napping."

"You're not napping if you're talking."

Muffled shuffling noises, then the click of the dead bolt being turned. The door opened a crack. "What?"

Well, that was an interesting question. Devin didn't actually have a reason for seeing her. Not right now, anyway. He had his duffel to unpack. The shower was beckoning. And she wasn't exactly brimming over with hospitality.

But if he let her shut that door, he might not see her for hours. And that just wasn't acceptable.

"Devin," she prodded. "What's up? Other than me?"

"Practice." It was the best he could come up with. Besides, it was true.

"Practice?"

"Right," he pushed the door open and walked in past her. It was unlikely she was going to rip off her clothes and jump into his arms, but neither did she look as though she was about to kick him out. A minor victory, but a victory nonetheless. "Television. This evening. Interview. Any of this ringing a bell?"

"Oh." She moved to the bed and stretched out, her back against the headboard, her chin resting in her hand. One finger tapped at her lip. "Afraid you can't handle the spotlight?"

He didn't hesitate. "Of course not."

She raised one eyebrow. "So confident?"

Was she challenging him? Why? Had she lost faith in his ability to play the part? She should know better. He could be Alexander. He would be anything she wanted him to be, as long as in the end she only wanted him to be Devin.

Alexander was suave, in control. And arrogant. Devin could do that. He crossed to the window, standing straighter than he usually stood, shoulders back and rigid. He searched for the faint British lilt to color his voice.

He turned to face her. "'*Confidence is the last refuge of the fool*,'" he said, bending forward into a regal bow, his head up and his eyes fixed on Paris. "'*And I assure you, madam, that I am a fool for you.*'"

"'*So confident that you will defeat me at my own game?*'" Paris said.

She was playing along, and the fact that he'd managed to lure a grin from her lifted his heart. Too bad it took his Alexander persona to accomplish that little feat.

In two long strides he reached her. He took her hand in his, then traced the tips of his fingers lightly over her palm, teasing, tickling. She closed her eyes, and he saw the struggle reflected on her face. He longed to kiss those little creases between her brows, to kiss the edges of her mouth, to coax away her frown.

He lowered himself onto the bed. When she opened her eyes, he put his arms out, urging her toward him. Her smile as she slid into his arms was shy, sweet, almost grateful. He could sit that way all day, her back pressed against his chest, his fingers linked with hers, their arms intertwined and wrapped around her chest. She belonged there, next to him. He'd known it the moment he had first seen her. Now he just needed to figure out how to make her realize it, too.

"Paris," he murmured, letting his lips dance over her shoulders, silently urging her to confide in him, to tell him her troubles and let him help.

She trembled, and pulled his arms tighter around her as she snuggled closer. He kissed the top of her head, breathing in the raspberry scent of her blond curls, then whispered, "'*I assure you everything will be all right. Sometimes the most catastrophic defeat renders the sweetest of victories.*'"

Her body stiffened against him, and she sat up, still in his arms, but no longer pressed against his back.

She had moved less than three inches, but now the Grand Canyon stretched between them. Devin didn't know what had caused it, and didn't have a clue how to bridge it.

"Paris?"

"You're fine. You don't need practice. Montgomery Alexander hardly needs to be coached on how to behave during an interview on the local news."

Lightbulbs flashed, thunder crashed, trumpets blared, the soundtrack surged. All the usual indicators. Realization finally hit. She was jealous. Stupid of him not to have realized before. She was jealous, and he was a fool.

Paris didn't want Devin. Not yet, anyway. Alexander was the one who had comforted her, who had touched her skin, kissed her hair. Paris sought refuge in Alexander's arms, not Devin's.

But even as she longed for Devin to transform into Alexander, warm and willing and so much more alive than her fantasies, she resented him. No, she resented the limelight that went along with his role. The very role she asked him to play.

His muscles tensed and his jaw tightened. The situation ate at his gut.

He got up from the bed and stalked to the window. Happily ever after loomed before him, big as life, on the other side of this book tour, and damned if he knew how to get there. In her mind, Devin was still just a slick streetcon. She'd fight like hell before she'd give in to just Devin.

But he couldn't sneak into her heart by starting out as Alexander, either. Not if she was going to be jealous and removed.

The scope of the problem frustrated him. He'd worked hard his entire life. Nothing had slipped from his grasp if he'd worked hard enough at it. Escaping his dad's lifestyle, taking night classes, opening his pub.

But he'd never wanted a woman like this before. And certainly not a woman like Paris. A diamond. Now that he did, knowing he might not be able to have her irritated the hell out of him.

With one hand, he pushed the curtain aside and looked down fourteen floors to Santa Monica Boulevard. He could see the ocean in the distance, the sun glinting off the dancing waves.

Devin wasn't a quitter. He'd beaten the odds before. And something told him that, deep down, Paris wasn't at odds with him. She was attainable. She just didn't know it yet.

Deep in his soul he knew that Paris was the woman for him, and that he was the man for her. Somehow, someway, he'd make sure she realized that as well.

In the meantime, he had no choice but to play the role he was hired to play—Montgomery Alexander. He'd just have to remind her that she was the one who'd hired him to play it.

PARIS WATCHED as Devin pushed the heavy drapes aside. The California sun spilled into the room, bouncing off his hair and dancing on the gold-flecked wallpaper. Usually a cheery room and sunshine lifted her spirits. Not this time. She knew she was being difficult, but couldn't help it. She wasn't sure if it was nerves or lack of sleep, the obnoxious bellboy or the gorgeous man in her room, but something in her was going ballistic.

Eternity passed before he spoke again. "You're right, Sommers, as usual. I don't need to rehearse. I could give an interview in my sleep." He turned away from the window and looked at his watch, his casualness irritating. "The studio's sending a car for us at five. I think I'll go hit a few bookstores. Sign autographs."

"Autographs?" Paris couldn't believe he had the gall to suggest that he should just go downstairs and start signing autographs. "Wait just a second."

She kneeled at the end of the bed, putting her just about eye to eye with him. "*I'm* Alexander," she said. "Maybe I should just go downstairs and announce it to everybody."

"Maybe you should." He opened his mouth as if to say something else, then closed it. For a second, she thought Devin was going to fight back. She almost hoped he would. Her insides felt all knotted up, and she wondered if some heavy-duty verbal sparring, followed by a crying jag, wouldn't make her feel better. But then Devin's face softened, and Paris knew she'd have to get through the afternoon without a tantrum. *Pity.*

"You're not really mad at me, you know." He paused, probably giving her a chance to agree or argue. He was right, but she didn't say anything. "You're really mad at yourself."

"Myself—"

He didn't let her finish. "I think you should go ahead and do the interview. Why not? Go ahead and reveal all."

Paris took a breath to calm down. How did she manage to get so worked up about one bellboy? Montgomery Alexander had lots of fans. She'd known that for years, and it had never bothered her before. At least not very much.

But none of those fans had closed an elevator door in her face.

She closed her eyes. No wonder she was cranky, what with lack of sleep and close quarters with an off-limits man who made no secret of the fact he wanted her. Who wouldn't be stressed?

She took another deep breath, then let it out slowly. "I'm not mad. Really." She caught his eye. "Besides, it's just for three more books and then it's bye-bye Alexander, hello my life."

He spun the desk chair around and straddled it, one leg on either side, his arms crossed over the top of the back. Forget cool, suave and sophisticated Alexander. He was one hundred percent Devin, masculine and casual and hot. She couldn't stop staring at him.

"Get rid of Montgomery Alexander and get your life? Seems to me like you've got a pretty good life right now." He tilted his head, as if recalling all the things she had going for her. "Steady income, a body of work you should be proud of and you're writing the stuff you enjoy."

Paris opened her mouth to respond, then closed it. The man was impossible. He had no clue what he was talking about. Really. Her life would be on track when she could do what she'd always planned on doing. The fact that she enjoyed writing the Montgomery Alexander books had nothing to do with anything.

"Well," she finally retorted, "at least bellboys won't snub me, and I won't have to travel the globe with race-track happy, casino-loving con artists." He flinched a little at that, and Paris almost apologized, but he'd started it, and *technically*, what she said was true. Besides, she was on a roll.

"Also, I can have a nice house and a study. Do book tours where I'm the one doing the signing and giving the interviews. I can visit my family without lying about my job, and, and..."

Paris stopped, sure that there was more, but not sure what it was. Right here, right now, none of her spiel sounded all that appealing. Certainly not as appealing as the prospect of the upcoming weeks with Devin. With his wacky sense of humor and laid-back manner, he was turning out to be a lot of fun.

Not to mention the added benefit of the way her heart skipped every time he looked at her. A perk, true, but still torture since his gaze was the only thing she intended to let caress her.

"Well, it sounds like you've got the whole thing worked out. I suppose you're right. I mean, what more could you want?"

There was nothing argumentative about his words, but Paris couldn't shake the feeling that he thought she wanted a lot more. Maybe he was right. Paris was beginning to think she didn't know what she wanted anymore.

"I'm sorry about earlier," she conceded. "Really. I was out of line. I hired you, and you're doing a fabulous job." She skimmed over every luscious inch of him and couldn't help but smile. "Truly fabulous." She cleared her throat. "So, are you going down to the bar?"

He flashed his killer grin. "Actually, I don't get to stay in hotels very often. I was thinking about doing something a little wild and crazy." In one motion, he pushed himself off the chair and held his hand out to her. "Care to join me?"

THE END CREDITS ROLLED, and Paris sniffed and wiped a couple of tears away. They were sitting next to each other on the bed, their backs against the headboard, the remains of cheesecake and apple pie littering the foot of the bed.

Devin passed her a tissue, an amused smile tugging at his mouth. "It was an action flick, not *Terms of Endearment.* Why are you crying?"

She shrugged. "I always cry. I cry at long-distance commercials. And those soup commercials," she clutched her chest, "those get me every time." She sniffled again.

"The perfect consumer." He passed her the entire box, then slid closer.

She leaned against him. "Thanks for a perfect afternoon." They'd done nothing except hang out in the room, but lazing around with Devin ranked as one of the best times she'd ever had.

"You're welcome." He urged her closer until her breasts pressed against his chest, and she realized her nipples were hard. Her body warmed as Devin's hands drifted along her back, and she noticed with mild surprise that her hands were exploring his shoulders, his neck, his back.

Her head screamed that she shouldn't be doing this, but she didn't care. All she wanted was Devin, the touch of his skin against hers, his breath mingling with hers.

"Paris?"

One glance up was all it took for the flames to ignite. She knew what he was thinking. What he wanted. She could hardly believe that he could need her as much as she needed him. But the desire was there in his eyes, and she pressed her body closer, longing to be a part of him.

She moved her lips up to meet his, then tasted the fire of his mouth. His lips parted and his tongue explored the soft corners of her mouth before demanding entrance.

A slight tug, and her shirt came untucked from her jeans. His hands stroked her back and up the sides of her body until his fingers were sliding under the thin material of her bra and cupping her breasts. She moaned, and his tongue thrust deeper, warm and wild and tantalizing. She greedily returned the kiss, her fingers running through his coarse, thick hair as she pulled his head down to force his kiss deeper and deeper.

She wanted more. So much more. She wanted all the things she knew she couldn't have with him.

Knowing she'd hate herself for it, she broke away. The hollow feeling in her stomach expanded the farther away she moved. But she needed to get away, needed to clear her head. She slid off the bed, moving to stand near the window.

"Guess we broke some ground rules, huh?"

Disappointment laced his voice, and she silently thanked him for not urging her to change her mind. "Guess so. Your hugs are lethal."

"Registered weapons."

But what a way to die. He was still sprawled on the bed, and she fidgeted. This was one of those moments Emily Post didn't cover.

"Well," he said, standing, "I guess I'll..." He cocked his head toward the connecting door.

"Right. It's almost five, anyway. We should get changed."

Pushing the connecting room door open, he said, "I'll be in here if you need me. Holler when the car comes for us."

As soon as the door shut behind him, Paris flopped backward onto the bed and pulled her pillow over her face. Then she let out a howl of frustration that could shake the heavens. With just a little concentration, Paris was sure that she could hear Rachel laughing on the other side of the continent.

Admit it. The only thing that's going to make you feel better is a roll in the hay with Devin.

Maybe so. But that still didn't mean she had to act on it. He was a guy she had no business even thinking about. A guy who'd almost blackmailed her. Who wandered around the streets of New York scamming innocent grandmothers. And children. And puppies.

She rolled onto her stomach, clutching the pillow under her. Except, she admitted, he didn't really seem the type. He owned a pub, after all, and from what she could tell, he spent a lot of time working there. So when did he find time to pull cons on blind Girl Scout leaders?

And he did walk away from what he'd planned for you.

She glanced at the closed connecting room door. As far as she could tell, he hadn't bothered to bolt it. Maybe...

Don't even think about it. Frustrated and hollow, she got up and paced. A week ago, she'd been perfectly content with the way her life was panning out. She had her fantasy in one corner, complete with the man of her dreams. In the other corner, she'd kept reality. A suitable man, a solid career, respect.

But now Alexander had walked into her life. Or at least the closest thing to Alexander in a living, breathing human. And everything had changed.

She flopped back down on the bed and hugged the pillow tight against her body. He was in her blood. Coursing through her veins. He was everywhere. In her thoughts, her skin, her pores, her essence.

Like water on a rock, he kept eroding her defenses.

Rachel would tell Paris to quit torturing herself and sleep with the man. To go ahead and squeeze that Charmin.

Use him the way he'd almost used her.

Or realize he has a permanent place in your heart. The little thought wormed its way into her head, and Paris pushed it away. That was one possibility she couldn't fathom. Not now.

But sleeping with him? Taking the proverbial bull by the horns? Maybe that wasn't such a bad idea. Her brilliant, professional-only plan had done nothing but leave her frustrated.

For three whole weeks she was going to be in close quarters with a man who'd come straight from central casting to play Alexander. He walked, talked and acted like her fantasy man, and she'd actually laid down no-touching ground rules. Was she nuts?

Most women would give up chocolate for the chance to spend three weeks traveling with the man of their dreams. Not her. Like an idiot, she'd made up rules. Rachel was right. She was acting like a martyr.

Well, no more. As soon as they got back from the interview, she'd make sure Devin realized the rules no longer applied.

"So, CAN I HAVE YOUR AUTOGRAPH? It's, uh, for my girlfriend." The twenty-something cameraman thrust a dog-eared copy of *Death in a Pretty Package* and a ballpoint pen toward Devin as he stepped off the slightly raised stage.

"Sure thing." Devin scribbled the signature he'd practiced in the hotel across the title page. "What's her name?"

The kid flushed as red as his hair. "Oh. Um, just make it out to Mark."

Devin looked down to hide his grin and added a personal note before handing the book back to Mark. "What did you think of the interview?" From Devin's perspective, it couldn't have gone any better. He'd come up with an answer for every question, managed to plug the current book quite a few times, bantered with the anchorwoman, and even hinted that a few fictional adventures were based on his experience as a secret agent.

He wanted to know what Paris thought, but since she was still in the control booth, he'd have to settle for Mark's opinion.

"Oh, man, you were awesome, Mr. Alexander. I mean, like, totally awesome. Just like your books." Mark clutched the paperback tight against his chest and looked down at the vinyl floor. "So, uh, can I, you know, ask you a question?"

"Of course," Devin said, remembering too late that a die-hard fan surely knew more about Alexander than Devin did.

"In *Angels and Assassins*, when Joshua's pretending to be the girl's long lost husband, what's his deal? I mean, is he really interested in her, or is he just trying to get close so he can steal the code from her boyfriend and disarm the bomb under the embassy?" The words spilled out, and when he was done Mark took a deep breath and looked up at Devin, apparently waiting for the famous author to spew nuggets of brilliant insight.

Devin kept a polite smile plastered on his face and tried not to grimace. *Angels* was one of Paris's older books, and he hadn't spent as much time studying her plot outline. But from what the kid had said, Devin was pretty sure he knew how Paris would answer. No, he corrected, he knew how he hoped she would answer.

"He was always interested. From the first moment he saw her. Even though he had to pretend to be someone else, his feelings for her were always true."

"Then it really sucked that she stayed with the boyfriend, huh?"

The arrival of the anchorwoman who'd conducted the interview saved Devin from having to explain why his reality didn't match the fiction Paris wrote. She stopped just long enough to shake Devin's hand one more time. "Fabulous interview, Mr. Alexander. We'd love to have you back when your next one comes out. Truly fabulous." With Mark at her heels, she continued toward the dressing room, leaving behind a wake of gardenia-scented air.

Awesome and fabulous. Devin grinned. These were adjectives he could get used to. Yes indeed, this celebrity thing was turning out better than he imagined. From the moment the interview started, Devin had to admit he'd actually missed the role-playing he'd done when he was pulling a con with his dad. He always knew he had a knack, but it never occurred to him that he might miss the creative rush that came with stepping into someone else's shoes.

And not only did he get to slide legitimately back into character, but he got to be a semi-famous author with a boatload of loyal fans. Not that the fans were really his. Paris was the real celebrity, and he was anxious for her verdict on his first solo flight as Alexander.

He glanced up toward the control booth and saw her step toward the glass. He waved, trying to stand out from the grips and gaffers cleaning up after the shoot. At first she didn't see him, but when her eyes finally met his she waved back, a smile springing immediately to her lips.

Unrehearsed, spontaneous, *real*. That one smile improved a day that Devin didn't think had any room for improvement. She pointed behind her, and Devin knew she was heading for the stairs. He stepped over the wires and cables and met her as she opened the control booth door.

"So how did Alexander do?" he whispered, slipping an arm around her shoulder.

"Alexander was amazing. Witty, charming, just a hint

of mystery. I couldn't have asked for better." She smiled up at him. "Thanks. You were brilliant."

Of course, she hadn't expected any less than brilliant. From her perch in the control booth she'd fidgeted through the entire interview, and not because she was nervous about the media. No, she was just anticipating *later*. Crossing and recrossing her legs had done little to dull the sweet ache that had been building in her ever since she'd decided to sleep with him. She'd missed half of the interview just because her mind kept wandering to fantasies of what she wanted to be doing with Devin back in their rooms.

During their return drive to the hotel Paris was sure she would spontaneously combust at any moment. Devin sat in the front seat, amiably chatting with the taxi driver who had caught his interview on the news. Just as well. If he'd shared the back seat with her, Paris was positive she would ignite into a blaze that only he could put out.

Now back in her room, she regarded his door. He'd gone in to change into jeans, and then they were supposed to meet and grab a bite in the hotel restaurant. But Paris wasn't really interested in fruits and vegetables. She had other nourishment in mind.

She hesitated, then forged ahead and knocked. When he opened the door, she just stared, with absolutely no idea what to say. Her fantasies of how the night would pan out hadn't included much dialogue.

"Hey," he said, leaning against the door frame, "we've got to stop meeting like this."

He had unbuttoned his shirt, and it hung open and untucked, revealing his taut chest muscles and a smattering of silky hair, all of which Paris found extremely distracting. "Um," she said, and then congratulated herself on her brilliant repartee.

Amusement lit across his face, and that was all it took to spark her vocabulary. "You could help," she said, "instead of standing there laughing at me."

"Help?"

"Yes, help. This isn't easy." She gestured between them. "You, me."

"What am I supposed to be helping you with?"

"I've decided to seduce you. I'd appreciate a little cooperation, please."

"Oh," he said, awareness rising in his voice. "In that case, let's make sure we get this right. Come on in." He stepped back so she could come into his room. His bed was rumpled, the sheets mangled on top of the mattress, and for some reason that made her feel better. On top of everything else involved in a seduction, she didn't have to worry about messing up the bedspread.

She sat down in the room's one chair, and he immediately laughed.

"What?" she asked, and when he looked at her, moving his gaze up and down, she realized she was sitting with her feet flat on the floor, knees together, her hands folded in her lap.

"You're not exactly posed for seduction."

Paris tried to loosen up, intentionally lifting one leg and crossing it over the other. "I'm still a little iffy on this seduction thing."

She watched his slow grin. "You're a cruel woman, Paris. Get my hopes up and then just dash them to the ground." He was on the bed, legs stretched out in front of him. Now he leaned back against the headboard, resting his head in his hands.

Hardly the picture of a man whose hopes for a wild night in bed had just been dashed. More like a fox who just realized he'd accidentally been locked in the chicken coop.

A very sexy, very smug fox.

She stood up. It was easier to focus when she was standing. "The thing is, if we do this…this…thing, it's not because there's anything permanent there." She stopped pacing in front of the bed and looked down at Devin, still reclining on the bed. So far he didn't look too concerned about her parameters.

"I've got a plan," she added, "for my career and my life."

"With those boring men you date?"

"What? Oh, you overheard me and Rachel. They're not boring. They're nice men. Doctors. Accountants. Investment bankers. Stable. Dependable."

He eased off the bed and stood up, just a footstep away from her, his six inches of height over her giving him the advantage. "But you're in here with me now," he whispered, as he took her hand and raised it to his lips.

Thinking was a problem. Coherent thoughts were dropping by the wayside. "Yes, well. That's the point. Now isn't later." She took a shaky breath. "It's just chemistry between us. It has to be. But there's no point in torturing ourselves for three weeks. We're consenting adults. We'll just have a little fun. An affair. A fling."

His lips grazed her palm. "I'm nice. I'm dependable. Respectable."

She made a soft noise in her throat. "Maybe. But you're…it's not the…" She took a deep breath. "If we do this, it's temporary. Just on the book tour. I just want to be clear on this. Up-front."

"Paris?"

"Mmm?"

"You're here with me now." He pulled her roughly to him, his mouth immediately capturing hers.

Slowly he released his claim on her lips, but one hand remained firm around her waist, pulling her close and pressing her into him, sending her mind reeling. His mouth played over her neck, and she threw her head back to let his lips dance on her flesh.

She pulled away from his kisses. "I want us to have an understanding, Devin," she murmured.

"There's something you should know."

She couldn't tell if he was teasing or not. "What?"

"I raised the money to buy the pub trading commodities."

Okay, he was teasing. She chuckled. First he adopts all of Alexander's traits, then he makes up characteristics of her not-really-boring dates for himself. The man was certainly willing to cover all aspects of her fantasies. But that didn't change the facts. "Are we clear? It's temporary?"

"Paris."

"Yes?"

He shook his head. "Never mind. I think we're clear." His gaze held her fast, the boiling desire she saw there enough to make her knees weak. "We're changing the ground rules from no sex, ever, to wild, hot, torrid, passionate sex as often as possible over the next three weeks. Is that right?"

Her body throbbed simply from his words. His eyes promised unimaginable pleasure, and she nodded agreement, unable to speak.

"Good." He kissed her fingertips. "But there's something I should warn you about."

Her chest constricted, and she tried to steady her breathing despite the way his lips brushed the tender tips of her fingers. She managed only a whisper. "What?"

His fingers grazed her cheekbone and dropped to caress her lips. "I intend to try and change your mind." He leaned in and she felt a whisper of a kiss on her earlobe. "I just thought it was fair to warn you, in the interest of full disclosure."

"Devin, I—"

He pulled her to him. His kiss, powerful and possessive, cut off speech and coherent thought until nothing was left in her except a wild hunger. She undulated against him, soaking up his heat, tasting the luxury of his hard, lean body.

With a boldness that surprised her, she reached down between their bodies and cradled his hardness in her palm. He shuddered under her touch, and his reaction sent her own passion soaring to new heights. She wanted him to shudder, to cry out in ecstasy, to find absolute pleasure in her touch.

His hands stroked her legs, and her skin began to burn up under her clothes. Her stomach tightened. A soft moan escaped her lips. She tilted her head back, needing to see passion reflected in his eyes.

"Devin," she whispered, "make love to me."

Uttering a deep, guttural groan, he pulled her with him to the bed, managing somehow to end up on top of her as they sprawled across the cool sheets.

"Close your eyes," he said, and when she did, he kissed each eyelid, a feather kiss rendered by firm and demanding lips. The rest of her body tingled in anticipation.

A flurry of sensation above her belt as a fingertip trailed lightly over her waist. The slightest of touches with the deepest of promises. When he started to peel off her clothes, she raised her hips in accommodation, until she was naked from the waist down.

"Can I open my eyes?"

He brushed a kiss across her lips. "No."

His lips burned a path down her neck to the collar of her blouse. His breath burned hot against her body. Her thin shirt suddenly seemed thick and cumbersome as a winter coat. "Just rip it off," she begged, when his fingers fumbled at the buttons.

"You're sure?"

"Please," she cried, her voice rasping from the need to feel nothing against her skin except him.

One tug and she heard the satisfying rip, felt the cool rush of air on her skin. Devin's hands cupped her breasts. When his tongue teased over her nipple, she pulled her legs together, tight, struggling to keep control. She reached up for him, but he pulled away, catching her hands.

"Not yet."

With one motion, he turned her over on her stomach, pulling her free of her shirt. She stayed still as he nestled himself against her, his arousal pressing into the back of her thigh. His tongue traced patterns on the back of her neck, sending bursts of ecstasy racing through her.

While his lips roamed her back and shoulders, his hand slipped down, caressing her bottom. She held her breath as he traced a path between her buttocks.

"Open your legs for me."

She moaned and spread her legs wider, wanting him to cool the burning inside her. His fingers slid inside her, and she cried out, pushing herself down harder, wanting him deeper. He was like a fire that was spreading through her being. A fire she needed and wanted. So much she thought she might die if he did anything so foolish as stop making love to her.

"Devin, please."

IT TOOK ALL HIS WILLPOWER not to explode when she said his name. She intoxicated him. No woman had ever had such an effect on him.

Agony. Not being in her was such sweet torture, but he wanted to savor these moments, to draw out her pleasure for as long as possible.

"Devin, I…"

"Trust me." He grabbed her hips and rolled her over, then balanced himself above her, awed by her response to him, so honest and intense. Her face was flushed, her nipples tight. When she opened her eyes and smiled, shy and trusting and hungry all at the same time, he knew that she would be his. She had to be. He couldn't bear the thought of anyone else touching her.

Her eyes raked over him, stopping where he strained against the slacks he still wore.

"No fair," she whispered.

He struggled out of his clothes, and lowered himself on her, needing to feel her body against his skin. His erection nudged between her soft thighs, and he fought not to lose himself.

He kissed her lips for the briefest of moments, then slid his kisses down her chest to her navel, where his tongue flicked over her bare flesh, hungry for the taste of her. He heard her small moan of surprise when she realized he wasn't stopping there.

"Devin…"

Heady from the desire rippling in her voice, he nibbled and licked and sucked her soft skin, concentrating his attention on the tender inside of her thigh. Her breathing was coming faster and faster, her little moans and sighs music to him.

He moved his hand down to cup her sex, then slipped his finger inside her, wanting to know how hot she was, how ready. For him. With his thumb, he stroked her sensitive nub and she writhed against his hand, calling out his name.

Desperate to taste her, he let his tongue take over where his hand left off, first flickering across her most intimate place, then deep and demanding. Her fingers curled in her hair, and he knew she had lost herself as he was lost.

Her body stiffened, tightened under him, and when she cried out in release, she pulled him up to her. He kissed her savagely, deep and hard, until she slid her mouth from his and breathed one word against his lips.

"Now."

Already he was on the edge, and that one soft word almost hurled him over. He moved away from her only long enough to sheath himself, then balanced over her, taking one sweet moment to memorize the passion in her eyes, the way her lips moved in silent urging. She opened her legs wider for him, the most compelling invitation he'd ever received. He entered her then in one hard thrust, trading control and reason for the silky, hot passion.

Nothing he'd imagined compared with the reality of being inside her. Her body clamped around him, milking him with the tiny spasms of a woman on the precipice.

Her hands rasped over his back, her fingernails razing across his skin, the added sensation increasing his need for her. She cupped his rear in her soft hands and pushed, urging him deeper inside her.

Devin needed no encouragement, he thrust deeper, harder, wilder, grinding against her. She matched his every move, raising her hips up to meet his. When her body tightened around him, he knew they wouldn't last much longer.

She cried out his name, her spasms demanding he join

her. He drove into her one final time, then felt his body explode, his own release coming all too soon and not soon enough.

He collapsed next to her, and she snuggled against him, her back against his chest. He draped an arm over her and played lazily with her breast, feeling a possessiveness toward her body that surely lacked political correctness. He felt like a caveman. He'd claimed her. She was his.

"We won't get much sleep if you do that," she said, as he pulled and teased her nipple.

"Sleep is an overrated activity."

She responded eloquently, scooting her hips back so that her rear pressed softly against his groin. Already he was hard again, and he rubbed himself against her, letting the passion build slowly.

His hand stroked her belly. He heard her whispered plea, "Again."

He'd never have thought himself capable, but her sweet demand spurred his passion, and soon he'd flipped her on her back. This time their coupling was rough and wild, passionate and needy, lightning-fast and totally satisfying.

She snuggled against him, her features soft, a dreamy look in her eyes.

"Devin?" she said, and he heard the haze of sleep in her voice.

"Hmm?"

"I think I like these new ground rules."

They made love twice more during the night. Both times she'd moved innocently against him. Her hand had brushed against his chest. Her arm had rested across his waist.

Immediately his body would react, and at his heated touch, she would wake up and slide into his arms, rubbing herself sleepily against him until he had to have her yet again. He just couldn't get enough of her.

By the time he could hear the bustle of the hotel staff in the hallway, Devin knew only two things for certain. He was going to get damn little sleep over the next three weeks. And he was hopelessly in love with Paris.

Now all he had to do was convince her she felt exactly the same way about him. Devin O'Malley.

9

"SO, HOW'S OUR LITTLE PROTÉGÉ?" Rachel asked.

Paris balanced the cell phone between her shoulder and her ear. "Fabulous, of course. Hold on a sec."

Across the crowded neighborhood bookstore, Devin sat behind a table highlighted by an enlarged poster of *Dearest Enemy, Deadly Friend.* He looked up from the book he was signing and flashed her a smile.

Just one smile, and suddenly Paris was rattled and weak-kneed like a schoolgirl.

Paris forced herself back to the phone call, turning away from Devin's table so she wouldn't get distracted again. "It's amazing. I just aim him at a camera or a bookstore or a journalist and, poof, instant Alexander. Every interview has gone over like a dream. Nothing rattles this man."

"Of course not. Didn't you invent him to be smooth, in control, a skilled operator under pressure?"

"Rachel..." Paris warned. She was in no mood to get into the Devin-Alexander thing. Over the past few days, Paris was beginning to think that maybe Alexander wasn't all she'd cracked him up to be. Sure, sophistication and a background in espionage could add a little extra zest to a relationship, but she couldn't really picture Alexander sitting cross-legged in front of the television, wearing nothing but ratty twill shorts and a tacky T-shirt, content just to hold her hand.

"Can you hold on a sec?" Rachel asked. "I've got another call."

"Sure," Paris said, turning back around to pass the time watching Devin. She grinned, remembering how thrilled he had been the night before when he'd discovered *Arsenic and Old Lace* in the late-night television listings. He'd suggested they cancel dinner plans at one of the chic new bistros in West Hollywood, and Paris had willingly agreed.

At one point Devin had slipped his arm around her shoulder, and she'd rested her head in the crook of his neck. They'd sat that way for a long time, with Devin lightly stroking her hair, while Cary Grant discovered that his little old aunts were mercifully murdering stray gentlemen.

Their gourmet dinner consisted of take-out pizza and wine from the hotel. They ate on paper towels and drank from the hotel glasses on top of the mini-bar. And after the movie, he'd kissed each of her fingertips, then moved on to kiss much more interesting places.

A glorious evening. And unlike anything she'd ever imagined with Alexander.

With Alexander, it had always been formal gowns and scotch on the rocks, satin sheets and cruise lines. She pictured Devin in black-tie and smiled. He could do formal with the best of them. But could Alexander go grocery shopping? Could he lounge around in sweats and play poker on the bed? She frowned. She'd never thought about it. Reality had never crept into her fantasies. Hell, until recently, her fantasies had never become reality.

So which guy was really more appealing? Especially when one of them had the added benefit of being flesh and blood?

But this is only a temporary fling. He's still all wrong, re-

member? Yes, she remembered. But it was becoming more and more difficult to recall why she'd been so gung ho on planning her life out forever.

Paris jumped as Rachel coughed into her ear.

"Paris, did you hear a word I just said?"

"What? No, sorry."

"I said that I saw both of you on one of the late-night talk shows last night."

"Both of us? Which show? We taped four yesterday afternoon."

Rachel gave a dismissive snort. "Who cares? The point is you two looked awfully chummy. Have you used up my supply yet? Need me to overnight you a truckload? Hot pink? Vibrant green?"

"Will you stop it?" Paris said, with less force than she'd intended. She hadn't planned to keep secret the fact that she'd made love with Devin, but somehow she'd never got around to confiding in her best friend.

"Now I know you're a martyr. It's obvious you're crazy about him."

Paris couldn't bring herself to form an argument. It was true. Rachel was right. She was crazy about him. But if she told Rachel they'd slept together, her friend would latch on to her "He's The One" spiel. And that was a place her thoughts had no business going.

"So, did you find out about the room situation in Vegas?" Paris asked, changing the subject and hoping Rachel took the hint.

"Yep. I talked to your publicist this morning. Everything's fine. You and the Boy Toy are in a suite. Since I'm neither the author nor the author's imposter, I'm in a regular room."

"Thanks for calling for me. And I'm glad you're able to come."

"You think I'd miss Vegas? Where they pay men to stand on the street wearing gladiator costumes? Of course I wanted to come. And I check in the day before you, so if you want I'll check Alexander's itinerary and make sure nobody screwed up the appointments."

"You're an angel." Paris checked her watch. An hour until the store closed, but the line for the autograph table was still long. "I'm gonna let you go."

"Paris, I've got one more thing. Just one word before you go."

"What?"

"Latex," said Rachel, and Paris heard her drop the phone she was laughing so hard. Shaking her head, Paris clicked the cell phone shut without even waiting for Rachel to recover.

The urge to spend some time alone with Devin was suddenly palpable, but it would be a while before she could scratch that itch. Judging by the number of people still in line, Paris figured she had about an hour's wait.

The bookstore had big, comfy armchairs placed strategically around the store, and Paris grabbed one near enough to Devin that she could keep an eye on him. They'd agreed on the first day of the tour that if he hit a snag, he could flash her a hand signal and she'd somehow rescue him. So far it hadn't been needed.

Paris grabbed her notebook computer from her tote bag and hauled it into her lap. She really needed to get some work done on *Distant Passages*. Determined to make progress on this epic she was writing, Paris flipped open the computer and switched it on. She booted up the file and put her hands on the keyboard, ready to crank out those award-winning words just as fast as her fingers could type.

Nothing came.

Okay. No problem. She reread the last chapter she'd written, figuring that would stir some creative juices.

Boring. And how did she expand on boring? She had no ideas. Nothing.

At least nothing for *this* book. Her head was overflowing with ideas for the next three Montgomery Alexander books. Some really innovative ideas. Brandon would be impressed. She'd have to remember to tell him what Alexander was plotting when she called in to give him a progress report on the book tour.

She turned her attention back down to her epic. The cursor blinked at her, and she scowled.

Giving in, she changed files and her fingers began to dance over the keyboards as she wrangled and manipulated Joshua O'Malley, super spy extraordinaire, and the other characters in Montgomery Alexander's fictional world.

She did a double take, looking back at the screen. It was *Devin* O'Malley. Joshua's name was *Malloy*. The man had completely infiltrated her imagination.

"Boo."

Paris jumped. She'd been so absorbed that she hadn't realized Devin had finished until he was leaning over her.

"Sorry," he added. "I thought you'd heard me."

"What time is it?"

"About six. They're closing up. Ready?"

Paris nodded and collected her things, following Devin to the front, and joining him in thanking the manager for all the work the store had put into the signing.

"Hey, people eat this stuff up," the manager said. "Adventure, sex, a touch of mystery. A little class. The books go like hotcakes. Hope you don't plan on stopping anytime soon, 'cause you sure would disappoint a lot of people."

Devin flashed an Alexanderish smile, then looked straight at Paris before turning back to the manager. "No, this is one project that I'm in for the duration. At least as long as circumstances allow."

An unexpected tug of melancholy grabbed her. *Circumstances* gave them just three weeks. And then they'd both get back to their lives apart.

For now, at least, she intended to enjoy having Devin around. In and out of her bed.

They'd rented a car, and Devin opened the passenger door for her, then slid in behind the steering wheel. "Where to?"

"Where? The hotel. We're hitting San Diego tomorrow and I haven't even packed."

"Our last day in Los Angeles and you want to pack? Just throw your clothes in a laundry bag and let the next hotel press everything."

She rolled her eyes. Typical guy.

He twisted in the seat to face her, sporting a lopsided grin. "Come on, Paris, you know you want to."

"I do?"

"Oh, yeah. You really do."

Of course she'd do whatever he wanted. How could she turn him down? "Well, then. Lead the way."

Devin maneuvered the car through the tree-lined Pasadena streets, finally ending up on one of Los Angeles's many freeways.

Paris was completely lost. "Where are we going?"

"It's a secret."

"Oh." She caught a glimpse of a freeway sign as they merged onto Interstate 10 and headed west. "If you go the other direction we can visit my dad." Odd to think that the same piece of road traveled all the way to Texas, within just a few miles of her father's sprawling Houston house, and then on even farther to the Florida coast.

Paris usually slept on road trips, but a cross-country jaunt with Devin would probably be a blast. She could imagine him telling funny little stories to pass the time, or singing along with the radio. Then there would be all those stops at motels along the way. Cheap wine and bed picnics and all the perks that she already associated with Devin and hotel rooms.

"Daddy'll have to spend the evening alone, I'm afraid." He took his eyes off the road just long enough to fix them on her. "I've got other plans for his darling daughter tonight."

He let go of the steering wheel and checked his left palm, then exited the freeway. Another glimpse at his hand, and he made a series of turns, finally ending up in a parking garage. "This looks like as good a place to park as any."

"Let me see your hand," Paris demanded.

Devin opened the car door. "Okay, everybody out."

Paris crossed her arms over her chest and sunk down into the seat. "I'm not going anywhere until you let me see your hand."

"Hmm. Really?" She nodded. "That's a shame," he said. "Because I plan on having a great time tonight." He stepped out of the car and turned around to face her. "Well, see ya."

Then he shut the door, and Paris watched as he ambled across the parking structure toward the stairs. She half considered staying in the car, just to show him. She contemplated the roof of the car and shook her head. Who was she kidding? Of course she was going with him.

She should have known better than to try and bluff Devin the Wonder Gambler. He was probably a whiz at poker.

Sure that she would be mercilessly teased, she climbed out of the car and scrambled across the parking lot.

He was waiting for her just inside the stairwell.

"A minute and twenty seconds. Truly your stamina is something to behold." He was razzing her, of course, and she playfully stuck out her tongue at him.

The thought struck her that somewhere along the line she'd begun to expect, *to count on*, his gentle teasing, their silly games. Standing in a grungy parking garage somewhere in Santa Monica, Paris felt more alive than she had in a long time.

Before she realized what she was doing, she stroked his cheek. Devin caught her hand and kissed her palm before pulling her into his arms. They'd shared bunches of glorious kisses, but, like snowflakes, each was unique, and she drew closer in anticipation of this kiss. First soft and sweet, then harder and deeper until she thought she would drown in it.

As his tongue explored her mouth, she settled into the kiss, savoring the way Devin's hands explored her back, gently pulling her to him. His mouth moved away from hers and he littered her face with feather kisses. His tongue played over her ear, and she felt her skin ignite and her stomach tighten. A soft moan escaped her lips and she pulled back to face him. She recognized the passion in his eyes.

"Told you we should have gone to the hotel," she teased.

He planted a soft kiss on the tip of her nose. "Ever made love in a stairwell?"

"Devin!" She hoped he was joking, because if he was

serious, she doubted she'd have the wherewithal to insist on more traditional surroundings.

Footsteps pounded on the metal stairs, and two teenage boys descended toward them, lost in an animated discussion of video games.

She cocked an eyebrow at Devin in an I-told-you-so sort of way.

He shrugged. "So, we'll keep our eyes open for a better staircase." He pulled his arm around her, and she snuggled close as the kids scampered past.

"Devin," she murmured.

"Hmm?"

"What's on your hand?"

With a chuckle, he presented her with his lightly fisted hand. She uncurled his fingers to reveal several lines written in black ballpoint.

"Directions from the bookstore to the beach?"

Devin bent to kiss her forehead. "We'd been to so many bookstores, I was afraid I wouldn't remember the way back. And I wanted to walk with you in the surf. I wanted to see you on the beach at sunset. I figured if we ended up lost, so would the moment."

Paris blinked back tears. That had to be the most romantic thing anyone had ever said to her. "Thank you," she said, as he pulled her in front of him and closed his arms around her. She buried her head in his chest, and sniffed. "And thanks for dragging me out tonight."

"Sweetheart, this night is just beginning."

THE MAN KEPT MAGIC in his pockets, Paris decided hours later, as they stood barefoot in the surf. How else could he make a night of late-night television seem like the best time she'd ever spent, and then twenty-four hours later turn around and hand her the entire universe on a platter?

He wrapped his strong arms around her waist and pulled her close to him, burying his face in her hair. They stood that way a long time, looking out at the ocean.

The sun had long since escaped beneath the horizon in a pyrotechnical display of pinks and purples and oranges. Paris even swore she saw the green flash. Scientists might insist the little pop of green that made up the last bit of light from the setting sun was nothing more than refraction and other characteristics of light. But Paris knew they were wrong. It was magic.

Devin had given her a magical sunset.

Now she leaned against him, feeling warm and safe despite an endless ocean spread before them and the unfathomable universe above. Billions of stars reflected on the gentle waves laid out like a blanket just for her.

"It's beautiful," Paris whispered, sure that she couldn't have imagined a more perfect night, or a more perfect man, even if she'd tried.

"Yes," he agreed. "You are."

She hugged his arms tighter around her, trying to memorize the moment. "We should get back."

"Is that what you want to do?"

"No. But we've got a long day tomorrow, and I actually have to work some on this trip."

He didn't argue, and she was grateful for that, fearing her resolve would melt if he kissed her one more time. Movies and television might suggest otherwise, but she was pretty sure the Santa Monica police wouldn't take any more kindly to finding a couple making love on the beach than in a stairwell.

Back at the hotel, they headed first to her room, their fingertips lightly grazing as they walked.

"Are you sure you don't want to have another film festival?" he asked. "I think there's an old Bogart film on tonight. You could work after."

Paris kissed his cheek, resisting the temptation he offered. "We've seen how much work I get done after. No, I owe Brandon a Montgomery Alexander synopsis. Plus, I'm anxious to work on *Passages*. The ideas just won't leave me alone." She stifled a grimace, hoping that maybe that little white lie would spur some creativity.

He brushed his fingertips lightly over her hair, tucking a strand behind her ear. "Well, let no one say I interfere with the creative process."

But he did. Once she sat down, she stared at the blank computer screen, thinking about Devin. The way his mouth curved when he smiled. The scalding heat of his hands on her body. The sensation of him deep inside her.

She gave up. Maybe she could work later. Right now she needed Devin.

When she pushed open his door, she heard the shower running. For a moment, she considered joining him, then had a better idea. After she pulled the covers down, she spread her jeans at the foot of the bed. Her T-shirt took a prominent place in the path from the bathroom to the bed. She hung her bra from the doorknob, and dropped her panties to the floor, right at the threshold of the bathroom.

Naked, she slid onto the bed. With the sheet smoothed beneath her, she leaned back against the headboard. Then, in case she alone wasn't incentive enough, she unwrapped the chocolate hotel candy and balanced it on her breast.

By the time he finished his shower, she knew she'd be hot and wet from nothing more than the anticipation of his touch. Truth be told, she already was.

THE COLD SHOWER wasn't doing a thing for him, and he shut the water off with a jerk. They'd been apart for maybe forty minutes, and already he was going nuts without her.

Truly and without a doubt, he'd gone completely head over heels for this woman. No great newsflash, true, but he also had a sneaking suspicion that Paris felt exactly the same way about him. She just wasn't ready to admit it.

That was okay. He could wait. Devin could be a very patient man.

At least most of the time. Right now, he wanted to slam through the door to her room and convince her with his kisses to toss work aside for one more night. As appealing as the thought might be, he quashed the idea. Except for the public appearances, he was practically on holiday. But this was a working trip for Paris.

He considered calling Jerry to check on the pub, but dismissed that idea just as quickly. So far, he'd checked in at least once every day of the tour, and not a thing had gone wrong. During the last call, Jerry'd griped and swore he'd quit on the spot if Devin didn't wait at least thirty-six hours before calling again.

That left packing or sleeping. A movie was out of the question. Not without Paris there with him.

Devin stepped out of the tub and wrapped the child-size towel around his waist. He'd seen a lot of hotel rooms and no one had ever given him a good explanation as to why the damn towels had to be so small.

He opened the door and stepped into the room, stopping when he felt something soft and cool under his foot. Panties. Strange place for her to have left them. Then he noticed the bra swinging from the doorknob.

Suddenly the evening had potential.

The path of clothes led to the prize on the bed, Paris, spread out like a temptress for him. Her dreamy eyes beckoned, urging him to lose himself in her. He groaned and stiffened under the towel.

A seductive smile eased across her face. She reached up and grabbed the headboard above her, arching her back so that her breasts lifted toward him.

When he noticed the candy, he came close to losing control.

"I realized you missed dessert," she purred in what he knew in his heart was a voice meant only for him. "Can I offer you a snack?"

He managed some feeble noise. Right then, at that moment, everything in his life depended on touching her. Urgency moved him toward her. He dropped the towel at the foot of the bed and straddled her.

His erection pressed against her belly as his mouth closed over her breast. The candy melted on his tongue, as he pulled and sucked until the chocolate was gone and she was moaning in his ear, begging him not to wait, not to stop, not to do anything except be inside her.

That was a demand he had no intention of denying. Positioning himself over her, he slid into her, relishing how hot and ready she was for him. She lifted her hips, urging him to take her harder. Devin cupped her bottom and raised her to him, pulling her against him with each thrust, wanting to touch the deepest places within her. He didn't want her to have any doubt that she was a part of him.

Her back arched down, leaving him with a stunning view of her body joining with his. The taut skin of her stomach flushed pink from their lovemaking, and her breasts, round and perfect, bounced with each powerful stroke. Her shoulders grazed the mattress and her head tilted back, golden curls splayed wildly across the pillow. She was beautiful. And for now, she was his.

She licked her lips. "Yes, now, please."

With one final thrust he took her where she wanted to go, her body quaking and trembling, tightening around him, as he lost himself and joined her on the far side of passion.

DEVIN WOKE WITH A START and his hand moved to the other side of the bed. Empty. He sat up, panic threatening, then fading when he noticed the crack of light where the connecting room door was slightly open.

He peered into the next room and saw Paris hunched over her computer, banging away at the keyboard.

"Paris?" he said softly, but she didn't look up. He walked up behind and peered over her shoulder. Random words jumped out at him.

Joshua Malloy. Greece. Vivian Jones. Stiletto.

"Paris?"

Her hand flew to the top of the notebook, slamming the screen down. Then she twisted in her chair to face him, a pretty pink blush consuming her cheeks. "Devin. Hi."

"I didn't mean to scare you. I woke up and I..." He trailed off, reaching out to stroke her hair. "I wanted you next to me."

She relaxed a little and smiled. "I woke up with all these ideas. For *Distant Passages*."

He frowned. "Going well? You were rather engrossed."

"Oh, yeah. It's really coming together."

He opened his mouth to argue. The page he'd just seen was not a literary saga of epic proportions. But no protest came out.

What was she up to? Devin wondered later, as they stretched out on the bed. Twice now he'd seen her working on a new Montgomery Alexander book, and twice she'd denied it. His glance at the screen tonight had been fleeting, but Devin had seen enough to know that there was a new woman on the scene. Vivian. She'd had a stiletto knife tucked into her boot, and stabbed some dissident general through the heart before he could stab Joshua.

Very interesting.

More so since Paris kept insisting that she was working so hard on her epic, that it occupied her thoughts totally, that she was overflowing with ideas for her great literary work. Clearly, Paris had fibbed. From what Devin could tell, she was overflowing with images of guns and knives, plots and schemes. Not historical sagas and prose worthy of the Pulitzer Prize.

An enigma, that's what she was. A woman who said she was proper, that she wanted the right kind of life and the right kind of man. That was all fine in theory. But what was "right" for Paris?

She might want to think of herself as prim and proper, but Devin knew better. Paris had a wild side, an impulsive side he found incredibly appealing. That side of Paris didn't balk at things like inventing Alexander. That side didn't hesitate to traipse all over the country despite her fear of flying.

That was the part of Paris that had flirted with him in the elevator, had kissed him with gusto in the bar, had relaxed in his arms watching a classic movie. And that part gave herself completely to him every time they made love.

No question, Paris was a woman who needed to take a good long look in the mirror. And Devin was just the guy to hold it for her.

Because with each passing day, Devin wanted more and more for her to see that his reflection was right there beside hers.

10

DESPITE UNEXPECTED TURBULENCE, she'd survived the flight from Los Angeles to Las Vegas. And even though the taxi driver seemed to confuse the Vegas Strip with the racetrack at the Indy 500, she'd survived the drive to the casino hotel as well. So Paris had no intention of collapsing in mortification now that she'd made it this far. No matter how many smirks and giggles the teeny-bopper clerk in the casino gift shop aimed in her direction.

Sure that she was blushing, Paris snatched her change and the paper bag, and headed out of the shop and back into the tacky opulence of the casino. Rachel skirted a cluster of polyester-clad women contemplating the slot machines and caught up with her, a wicked grin plastered across her face. She snatched the bag and peered inside. "Well, well."

"It's not what you think," Paris said.

"A twelve-pack, no less. Did you get fluorescent? Ribbed? Tell me you at least bought extra large."

"Rachel!" Paris came to a standstill, glancing around to make sure no one, especially Devin, was listening. "You're such a—"

"I know. I am. It's true." The smile returned. "Come on. Give. Or I'll just jump to my own sordid conclusions."

Paris allowed herself a tiny smile. Any more self-satisfied and she could pose for Da Vinci. The surprising thing was that in just a few days she'd gone from wanting to keep her secret all to herself to wanting to tell. "It's not what you think. What *do* you think?"

"That since you're in Las Vegas, land of lust, you finally got smart and decided to jump his bones. I only hope that you at least wait until you're in your room. Casino security frowns on that kind of thing." She leaned forward. "And they have cameras. If you're not careful, you'll end up in the sale rack at Big Barney's Triple-X Playhouse."

Paris rolled her eyes and pulled Rachel behind a bank of slot machines.

"Are we doing espionage?" Rachel quipped.

"I told you it isn't what you think," Paris sang. She watched Rachel's eyes widen at the scent of gossip.

"What, then?"

"You think I'm planning a seduction."

"Yes. Either that or it's his birthday and you're buying really unique balloons."

"Too late."

"Too late, what? His birthday?"

"Seduction, stupid."

Rachel's eyes widened. "No way. You and the Boy Toy? That's fabulous." Her brow furrowed. "It was fabulous, right?"

Paris laughed. "You are not getting the prurient details. But yes. It was. It is."

"Is? I guess you're expecting some encores, huh?"

"There've already been a few encores." She counted on her fingers. "A few in Los Angeles, a few in San Diego, a few in San Francisco. And I plan to make the most of this last week. Like you said, we're both adults."

"And you've both got the hots for each other."

"Temporary hots," Paris said. "We made a deal." A deal that was for the best. Long term with Devin would be a mistake, no matter how wonderful short term might be.

"So you're both just going to walk away after the tour?"

"Right." Paris saw Rachel fight back a grin. "What?"

"Nothing. It's just that we're in Vegas, the land of gambling. I'm thinking surely I can make some bucks off of this, 'cause sweetie, you are so going to crash and burn."

"No, I'm not," Paris insisted.

"You really shouldn't bet against me," Rachel said, casually examining her nails. "So far I've been right on the money."

"You're infuriating."

"I know." Rachel searched the cavernous room. "So where is your little love toy?"

Paris decided to let the "love toy" comment slide. Besides, she kind of liked the sound of it. She stepped back from the slots and turned in a circle, but didn't see Devin either. "He's here somewhere. After we checked in, he said he was going to look around the casino."

"Do you think that was a good idea?"

Paris shrugged. "Why not?" And then she remembered. Twenty thousand. Gambling debt. Had she actually let him loose in the candy store?

She reached out and grabbed Rachel's arm. "You've got to help me find him."

Finding one man in a crowded casino in Las Vegas was not as easy as it sounded. After an hour, she'd still come up with no sign of Devin.

She found a bar tucked in a corner near the blackjack tables, and plopped herself down on a stool. She ordered a glass of wine and wondered if Rachel was having better luck.

And then she saw him, right there in front of her.

She stood up, then realized she was looking at a mirror. Spinning around, she tried to find him behind her.

Nowhere. The stupid mirror was at an angle, and was

reflecting an image from yet another mirror. And Devin must have moved, because now he wasn't even part of the reflection. But he was nearby. That much was certain. Unfortunately, the bartender had also disappeared, so she couldn't pay her bar tab.

Cursing mirrors and bartenders, she plunked a ten dollar bill on the bar, blew off getting change, and set out to comb the area. She'd either find him, or she'd hire a mathematician to analyze the angle of that stupid mirror.

Paris passed behind a pillar, mirrored of course, and stopped short.

"Counting cards isn't going to make you a success, Andy, any more than hanging out at the tracks back home," she heard Devin say.

"Carmen says I've got a knack for cards."

Paris inhaled sharply, then clapped her hand over her mouth, afraid Devin might hear her. This Andy kid sounded much younger than twenty-one. What was the kid doing in a casino?

"I'm not surprised," Devin said. "You're a smart kid."

"Damn straight," Andy said, a cocky edge to his voice.

"You could do a lot better than spending the rest of your life gambling or working for Carmen."

"My uncle Carmen's not a loser."

"I didn't say he was," Devin said, his tone level and reasonable. "But the people he works for are scum. You could do a hell of a lot better."

"He wants to talk to you. Wants to make sure you're not taking the extra time he gave you and running out on him. He told me to remind you of the package I dropped off at your place a few weeks ago. He said that should convince you not to blow him off."

"Where is he?" Devin asked, and Paris shuddered from the ice in his tone.

"Over there. Waiting for you."

"Andy, you don't have to live like this, you don't have to grow up to be a strongman for your uncle. You're smart. Finish high school and go to college. Then decide. At least then you'll know what your options are."

"You are so lame, man. You don't know what you're talking about."

"I do know. Just think about it."

Silence.

"Okay?" Devin pressed.

"Screw you."

Paris saw the kid as he walked by, head down, hands jammed deep into the pockets of his black leather bomber jacket. She wondered if Devin really saw the kid, or if he just saw himself years ago.

"Damn," Devin groaned, then he must have slammed his fist against the pillar, because Paris felt the reverb as she leaned against the mirrored surface. Her eyes brimmed with tears, and she knew what Devin was thinking. That kid wasn't going to give school another thought.

But at least Devin had tried.

Without thinking about what she was doing, Paris stepped around the pillar. She wanted to hold him, to comfort him, to tell him he'd tried his best and maybe he'd made a dent in the kid's armor. But he'd moved away. He walked in crisp, determined strides toward two burly men, one with a jagged scar on his cheek. Carmen, surely, and someone else.

She couldn't hear what they were talking about, but she could tell Devin was furious. He stood rigid, his hands clenched in fists by his side. The man without the scar finally stuck his hand out. Devin put his hands in the pocket of his jacket. The man with the scar said something and poked Devin's shoulder. Devin shrugged away from the touch as the other man thrust his hand out once again.

Slowly, defiantly, Devin faced each of the men, then turned his back to them and walked away.

"You remember what I said, Devie-boy," shouted the man with the out-thrust hand. "You know I'm a man of my word."

Paris slipped away to the other side of the casino before Devin could see her.

"Devin," she called out when she saw him pass nearby, "over here."

"Hey there," he said, and after a moment, he smiled. "You're a sight for sore eyes."

"Yeah? Why's that?" Paris asked, hoping he'd tell her what the tête-à-tête with the gorilla twins had been all about.

Devin just shook his head. "I've been wandering around, lost in the crowd. Nice to see someone familiar." He grinned, and this time it seemed genuine. "Especially someone so pleasantly familiar," he added, then kissed her gently on the back of her hand. A sweet, gentle gesture, and Paris felt her heart swell.

"I was going to find Rachel and get some lunch. Want to come?"

"I'm not really hungry yet. You girls go on ahead. I think I'll hit the blackjack tables."

"The tables?" Paris squeaked, then coughed. "You're going to the blackjack tables?" After that lecture he'd given the kid, Paris couldn't believe Devin was going to dive headfirst into gambling.

Devin shrugged. "I'm in the mood for some mindless entertainment." He leaned over and gave her a quick kiss on the cheek. "I'll catch up with you in a couple of hours," he said, stepping away.

"Wait!" Paris caught up with him. "Uh, wait a sec, Dev."

He turned, a question in his eyes. "Do you want to come with me?"

"Do you think this is such a good idea?"

He looked at her like she'd lost her mind.

"I mean, well..." Paris drifted off. How did she politely point out that racking up another gambling debt probably wasn't such a great idea?

Inspiration hit. "We need to get you prepared for tomorrow. Do you really think we can spare an hour while you play at cards?"

His brow furrowed and he regarded her through squinted eyes. "I thought you were off to have lunch."

Yup, she'd said that all right. *Now what?* "Right," she said, regrouping. "Right, I did say that. And we are. Yes. Lunch. Oh! We'll take it upstairs, and work while we eat."

"Uh-huh." He crossed his arms over his chest. The corner of his mouth curled up, and Paris couldn't decide if he was hiding a smile or rehearsing his speech to have her committed.

She waved her arm toward the elevator banks. "So? Are you coming?"

"No."

"No?"

"No," he repeated, still fighting a grin.

Well, shoot. She gnawed on her lower lip as she scoured the room with her eyes, hoping to find something, anything to get him upstairs. "Why not?"

"We've been over everything a hundred times. The last two weeks went off without a hitch. I think we can spare an hour."

She remembered the financial magazines he was always thumbing through and decided to try another approach. "Did you really buy the pub with money you'd made in the market?"

He leaned back against a slot machine. "Looking for stock tips?"

"Just curious."

"Didn't that kill the cat?"

He wasn't even trying to hide his grin anymore. Infuriating, really. He wasn't helping her in the least. She stood straighter, huffing up a bit. "I'm trying to have an interesting conversation and you're teasing me."

"Yes, I am."

"Devin!"

He leaned over and kissed her nose. "You're cute when you're annoyed."

Paris tapped her foot and glared.

"Okay, I surrender." He grinned at her. "Now I've forgotten the question."

Had she said infuriating? She'd meant exasperating. And irritating.

And fabulously handsome, but that really wasn't the point.

She blinked and frowned at him for getting her off track. "I asked if you really made money in the market."

"Yes. It's true. I took every night class I could find to learn about investing. College credit, extension, informal classes. The works. Surprised?"

"Not at all." Devin had drive. He was smart. She didn't doubt that he could do anything he wanted.

"Why do you ask?"

"I guess trading in the market is a little like gambling, don't you think?"

He shrugged. "I suppose. A little. But at least you can study the markets, reduce your risk."

"Right. Exactly."

"Right, exactly, what?"

"Well, if you were to lose, say, twenty-or-so thousand dollars in the market, that would be a pretty big thing to recover from, wouldn't it?"

"Twenty-or-so..." Devin trailed off, then cocked his head, looking at her. He put his finger against the side of his mouth and tapped lightly.

"You know," he finally said, "burning off steam at the blackjack table may not be such a good idea after all." He reached over and trailed his finger in gentle strokes up and down her arm. Tempestuous heat reeled through her. All it took was a look, a touch, and she melted.

"Uh-huh." She yanked herself out of dreamland. Now wasn't the time to get all hot and bothered. She needed to keep her mission in mind. "I mean, good. Good idea."

There was no reason on earth why such a smart, focused man couldn't fight the urge to gamble. And she'd do anything she could to help.

He flashed a lopsided grin. "Roulette would be much better. Even more mindless. Pure chance."

Plan B. She needed to come up with a Plan B.

She could think of only one surefire way to keep his mind away from gambling. Luckily, Plan B had benefits for her as well.

Calling up a sultry smile, she moved closer, then ran her finger along his collar. "The thing is, I'm not really all that interested in rehearsing or in having lunch."

"No kidding?" The look in his eye told her Devin knew exactly what she was up to.

"No, I'm much more interested in betting on more pertinent things. Like exactly how hot I can make you with just my mouth." She leaned in closer and flicked her tongue along his ear. "And I promise you that my odds don't favor the house."

He swallowed, and she knew she'd won that battle. When they got to the room, the actual war promised to be a lot of fun.

In the elevator, Devin grabbed her around the waist, and pulled her toward him. "It occurred to me that we never got to finish what we started on that elevator in New York."

"Oh, really?"

A trill of excitement coursed through her, growing stronger as he reached down and stroked the back of her leg, starting with her knee. His touch was light, teasing, so soft that it was little more than a caress.

When he reached her hem at mid-thigh, he pulled her in closer to him, until their bodies were melded together. There was no mistaking his arousal, and as he pulled her tighter against him, Devin slipped his hand up the back of her thigh, higher and higher under her short skirt until his finger grazed the edge of her panties.

Madness loomed before her, complete and utter insanity brought about by the torment of his touch.

"Devin. What if somebody...?"

"Do you want me to stop? Say yes if you do," he whispered.

"I... I..." She couldn't say it. And she didn't want to.

"Too late," Devin said, then kissed her hard on the mouth. His hand continued to explore, bedeviling her, as she squirmed under the pleasure of his touch.

"You do things," she whispered, "to my control. My willpower."

He traced the edge of her ear with his tongue. "Good. I've got more things in mind when we get to the room." As if to give her an idea of what kind of things, he slipped his finger inside her, silencing her cry of surprise and delight with his kiss.

The elevator glided to a halt, and in one fluid motion, Devin pulled away from their embrace. He stayed next to her, his arm around her waist, and she leaned against him, anxious to reach their suite.

The doors slid open and Devin led Paris past an elderly couple waiting to get on. Paris stared at the floor as she stepped out, sure that her face was bright crimson. The instant the doors closed behind them, Paris turned to Devin and laughed, a mixture of anxiety and relief.

"Do you think they knew?"

"No," he shook his head and kissed the tip of her nose. "And if they did, they were just jealous."

It took an eternity for him to get the door unlocked. Probably her fault, really, since he kept fumbling with the card key every time she rubbed her hand down his groin or licked the back of his ear. The second the lock released, he threw the door open, pulling her in with him.

"Now," he growled, pressing her roughly against the wall. He dropped his slacks and had her panties down before she had realized what he was doing, then he grabbed her waist and lifted her. "Put your legs around me," he said. Paris did as he said, arching her back so that her shoulders pressed against the wall.

He entered her like that, and the passion was devastating, like bottle rockets and starbursts. Paris cried out and wrapped her legs tighter around him, never wanting the moment to end, but afraid she might die if it went on any longer.

When she opened her eyes, he was smiling at her. She leaned forward and wrapped her arms around his neck as he readjusted his hold on her. "Wow," she whispered, wondering how this man could have come to mean so much to her so fast.

"Yeah," he said. "But..."

"But?"

"I can still hear those tables calling."

"Really," she said, throwing a tone of mock horror into her voice. "Well, maybe it's time to test my little wager." She nibbled on the side of his neck, her fingers unbuttoning his shirt. "Gentlemen, place your bets."

By the time her kisses reached his waist, she knew he was fighting for control. As she drew him into her mouth, he groaned and called out her name.

When she took him to the brink, he pulled her off and tugged her down to the floor. He entered her quickly, and she gasped when he shuddered inside her and collapsed next to her on the rough carpet.

"I think the house won that bet," he said.

Paris snuggled closer and ran her hand over his chest, twisting her fingers in his hair. "If you feel like placing another bet..."

She smiled and let her hand roam lower. Soon enough, they went from fireworks in the hallway to candlelight and roses in the bed. Intense and sweet, powerful and tender.

Afterward, Paris snuggled against him. Vegas and Texas. The last week of the tour. The last week of their deal. In seven days, he would go back to being Devin full-time, and she'd have her book deal and could get on with her life.

Her life without Devin. No wonder she felt melancholy.

She reassured herself that the deal she'd made with Devin was for the best. She had a specific life plan, and they were so different. Weren't they? Just because he made her feel alive, just because he made every moment special, that didn't mean she should abandon everything she'd planned. Did it?

She pushed the thoughts away, determined not to think

about it. Instead, she pressed herself tighter against him, coveting his warmth, especially now that their last day together was drawing closer.

She remembered the men in the casino. He still hadn't mentioned them. Was the uncle Carmen that kid mentioned the one to whom Devin owed the money?

"Devin," she murmured, rolling over so that she could look at him. "I saw you downstairs talking to some men."

Was that fear she saw in his eyes? "You did?"

"I waved from across the room, but you didn't see me."

"Sorry."

Something was wrong, but Paris couldn't get a handle on it. "It's no big deal. Who were they?"

"Just some people I know from New York. Coincidence bumping into them all the way out here."

On top of the possibility that Devin owed those creeps money, another problem occurred to her. "They know you?" What would happen if they saw him spending the week in Montgomery Alexander mode?

He must have understood. "Oh, they're on their way out of town tonight. Don't worry. They won't blow my cover." He kissed her, then pulled back and locked his eyes on hers. "I promise you."

She gave him a quick kiss on the lips. "I'm not worried. I trust you."

Devin sighed and rolled onto his back. "Why don't you just come out of the closet and confess to writing the Montgomery Alexander books?"

Paris propped herself up on one arm, studying him. "Where did that come from?"

"I was just wondering," he said simply.

What was going on?

She rolled over and lay back down, staring up at the ceiling. "I thought I already explained that to you."

He scooted next to her and sat up, leaning over her and looking down into her face. There was concern in his eyes. For her? Did he fear she was making a mistake with her life, her career? Or was there something more there?

Tenderly, he stroked her cheek. "Explain to your father that you love writing these books. I've read all of them. And sure, they're over-the-top, but the themes are all honorable. Courage and loyalty and patriotism. Your characters are strong. They're self-sufficient and smart. If he doesn't see that, then he's the one who's blind."

"It's not just my father. The fans love Alexander's image. I can't just step in and say it was me all along. Maybe if I'd done that from the beginning and had just invented a co-author. But not now. It's too late." She winked at him. "Besides, I'd get laughed out of town. Who'd believe me as Alexander? Who could after seeing you?"

He brushed a light kiss over her forehead. "Then don't tell the world. Just tell your father and forget about this literary epic idea. That's not you, no matter how much you think he wants it to be."

She started to argue, but he hushed her with a gentle finger on her lips. "I've seen you at night. I know about your new character, Joshua's new partner, Vivian, and her stiletto blade. I've watched you with your eyes closed as you make up new adventures. You're beautiful when you're working. You're alive because you love it."

Paris felt her eyes foolishly brim with tears. Stupid, really. She had nothing to cry about. "I'm just not used to writing in another style, that's all. I'll love that as much when I get good at it."

He kissed her then, and she took the kiss greedily, as if he were a fountain and she was drinking in his strength and courage. When he broke from the kiss, he looked deep into her eyes, silent, for a long time, so long that she began to squirm under his demanding gaze.

"Promise me something, Paris."

"What?"

"Just promise," Devin insisted.

She lifted a shoulder. "Okay, I promise. What?"

"Do what your heart says is right."

She frowned. Was he talking about her books? Or about him?

And more important, had she just made a promise she couldn't keep?

DEVIN OPENED HIS EYES and stared at the ceiling. He knew he was grinning, but he couldn't help it. Despite the visit early on from Andy's uncle Carmen and Bull, the last four days in Vegas had been a dream. Letting Paris continue to believe the twenty-thousand-dollar gambling debt was his, and not his father's, had been a stroke of genius.

Paris had been more than willing to abandon the casinos in order to keep Devin away from those demonic blackjack tables. He'd known exactly what she was up to, and she knew that he knew. And, of course, that made it all the more fun.

For the entire week, whenever they weren't working, they'd been in the hotel suite, sipping wine, watching movies. Making love. Glorious, satisfying, over-the-top love.

Devin felt a little guilty, sure, but not enough to own up. He'd never said the debt was his, after all. She'd only assumed. And the proper time to put his real cards on the table was after he was sure she'd admit to being head over heels in love with him.

He rolled over and kissed her cheek, then slid out of bed and padded toward the bathroom for a shower. He pictured Paris naked under the stream of water, slick with the strawberry scented shower gel the hotel replenished daily. For a second, he paused and considered waking her, but then dismissed the idea. He'd kept her up way too late the night before—he grinned at the memory—and they had a long couple of days ahead of them. A two-hop flight to Dallas, five bookstores to hit and drinks and cocktails with various reporters. Fly to Austin the next morning and repeat the process. Then Houston, and six more bookstores.

And looming at the end of all that was the party. Thrown by Paris's father, the federal judge.

The chasm between their upbringings mocked him, reminding him that Paris had insisted their arrangement be only temporary. He was playing way out of his league. And even if her dad liked him, that didn't change anything. Judge Sommers wasn't meeting Devin. Montgomery Alexander would have the pleasure of his company.

A hell of a mess.

He cast one last glance at Paris before closing the bathroom door. Somehow she'd managed to cocoon herself in the sheet, except for one leg that dangled over the side. He shook his head, smiling. He'd been right. She was a notorious covers stealer.

A needle-fine spray of water worked the kinks out of Devin's shoulders and back. He hoped he'd done the right thing in not telling Paris about Carmen's threats.

He was furious that Carmen had dragged Andy into his life-style. The kid was smart. He deserved better than to grow up thinking Carmen's way was the best way. Carmen and his flunkies sure as hell weren't going to let the boy expand his horizons.

Bastards.

They'd seen Devin on television and pried the whole

story out of Jerry. Devin couldn't blame Jerry, who'd spewed apologies for not keeping a lid on the secret. Devin knew just how persuasive Carmen and his lackeys could be. He was just grateful Jerry escaped with little more than a few bruises.

To think that Devin had actually believed he was nearly free from Carmen. With the money he'd get from Paris for playing Alexander plus the money Jerry'd been able to round up from friends, he had enough cash to satisfy his dad's debt.

Then Carmen had thrown in the monkey wrench, threatening to reveal Paris's secret unless she agreed to pay monthly hush money. Devin had said Paris didn't give a rat's ass about anonymity, that she'd reveal the truth herself rather than pay them.

It was a big lie, a whopper, and Devin hoped it wouldn't come back to bite him.

He adjusted the showerhead to shoot thick, massaging pulses, letting the water pummel his chest and face. He hadn't heard another peep from the hometown thugs. Maybe his bluff had worked. That was fortunate, considering he'd struck out trying to convince Paris to come clean with Alexander's fans, much less with her father.

Her father. Forty-eight hours before he met the man, and already Devin's nerves tingled. He decided to stay in the shower a few minutes longer, letting the powerful spray soothe his nerves and hoping it would wash away any sign of Devin's heritage, his neighborhood or his upbringing.

11

"YOU MUST BE MONTGOMERY ALEXANDER," the judge said, extending his hand. "Patrick Sommers. I'm so pleased you could make it to Houston. It's an honor having you in my home. And it's a pleasure to finally get to meet the man who's been keeping my little girl so busy." With his free arm, the judge gave Paris's shoulder a squeeze. She smiled at her father and looped an arm around his waist.

"The pleasure is mine," Devin said, with an Alexander-ish tip of his head. He liked the man already. Paris might fear that her father wouldn't approve of her life-style, but Devin would be willing to bet that Judge Sommers would forgive Paris just about anything.

Rachel elbowed in and planted a quick kiss on the older man's cheek. "So, where's the bar set up?"

The judge laughed. "It's good to see you again, too, my dear." He looked over his shoulder. "Catering is set up in the guest house."

Rachel grinned at Paris. "See, this is why I love visiting your dad. He understands my basic needs."

Paris raised an eyebrow. "Try not to single-handedly triple the bar tab, Rach."

"I'll do my best. But since you two got us here an hour late, I've got some serious catching up to do." She slipped into the crowd and headed for the quaint stone guest house.

Paris winked at Devin and then looked up at her father. "Making up for lost time."

Devin could see bits of Paris in the trim, distinguished man. Like his daughter, Patrick Sommers's facial features were well-defined. But it was their eyes father and daughter shared most prominently. Deep brown eyes that held infinite potential. Warm and welcome one minute, sharp and commanding the next.

"I read one of your books last night," Judge Sommers announced, looking straight at Devin.

Paris whipped around to face her father. "No way. Really?"

"What did you think?" asked Devin. He saw Paris stiffen, and he resisted the urge to take her hand and give it a reassuring squeeze.

The judge pulled at his chin. "Not my cup of tea, really," he said. Paris's shoulders slumped and she closed her eyes. "But," the judge went on, "it was quite a bit more entertaining than I had imagined. Well-written, the characters weren't flat. Moved quickly. It wasn't..." He seemed to be searching for an appropriate word.

"Trash?" Devin suggested.

"Ah, there you go," said the judge, giving Devin a chummy pat on the arm. "It wasn't complete trash."

"Trash? *Complete* trash?" Paris repeated, looking from Devin to her father and then to Devin again.

Devin laughed, and Paris glowered at him.

The judge squeezed her shoulders. "Calm down, honey. The author over here is laughing. I don't think I've offended your client." He cocked his head toward Devin.

"I'm not offended in the least," Devin said, sure that Paris was seething.

"There. You see. You never expected me to love his stories, did you?"

Paris sighed. "No, Daddy. I never did."

"Well, then. Why don't you two go join the party. Larry was looking for you earlier. I imagine he'll want to claim a dance."

"Larry?" Devin asked, as they walked away.

"We went to high school together. He's a federal prosecutor, and he just got appointed to head up the racketeering division. He's the youngest person ever to have that job."

Great. His competition was Larry the child prodigy. "Yeah. They asked me to do that, but I told them I really couldn't fit it in. What with my busy schedule and all."

Paris bumped him with her hip, laughing. "You behave."

"Make me," Devin teased, longing to pull her close to him, but remembering that he was in Alexander-mode. He crooked his arm and offered it to her, pleased just to have her by his side. They strolled through the stone-paved backyard, shaking hands and making small talk with the guests, who ran the gamut from staid professionals to multi-pierced college students. The party was a welcome home for Paris, but it was also the last stop on Alexander's whirlwind tour, so fans and booksellers and the media were noshing with judges and CEOs.

"This is an amazing house," Devin said, grabbing a seat on a marble bench next to the Koi pond. "Did you grow up here?"

"Pretty much. We moved here from our ranch after junior high." She waved her arm to encompass the magnificent, landscaped backyard. "This was just dirt and grass when we moved in." Now it was a paradise. Ivy crept up the fence, roses climbed trellises, cobblestones wound a path through sections of the garden.

Strings of ornamental lights laced the trees, and their

soft glow accentuated Paris's hair and skin. "You're beautiful," Devin said, particularly enjoying the way the crisscross halter of her silk dress accentuated her breasts.

"I bet you say that to all the girls," Paris said, her voice light.

Devin ached to kiss those lips, to taste her again. It had been over two hours since he'd held her close and kissed her, and that was two hours too long. "Paris, tell your father. Tonight. Follow your heart. Do it while we're here. He seems like a nice man, surely it won't be the explosion you think."

He felt her stiffen, and regretted pushing her.

"You tell me to follow my heart, but that's just the same as Daddy. He says to do one thing, and you say to do another."

"No, it's not the same," he said, more sharply than he intended.

Rachel sauntered up the walk, a fellow who looked as though he'd stepped off the cover of *Esquire* on her arm.

"Larry here asked to come see the lady of the hour."

"I thought we could have a dance, catch up on old times," said the child prodigy turned cover model.

"I, um," Paris looked from Devin to Rachel.

"Come, dance with me," Rachel insisted, holding out her hand to Devin.

He hesitated, seeds of jealously starting to take root.

"Come on. Let the kiddies chat. I don't bite. Not hard, anyway." She turned to Paris. "May I borrow him?"

Before Paris could answer Devin found himself on the dance floor.

"Well, you're tense as a board," Rachel said. "Feeling a little competitive, are we?"

"What? No," Devin said, far too quickly to fool someone as sharp as Rachel.

"Uh-huh," Rachel said, as she twirled into Devin's arm. "So, have you told her?"

"Told who what?" asked Devin, figuring that if she was going to drag him away from Paris, the least he could do was make her work for her information.

"You're a man in love, my friend. Have you told her yet?"

That one was out of left field, although he should have seen it coming. He'd spent some time with Rachel over the past week, at least enough to learn she didn't pull any punches. If what Paris said was true, Rachel didn't have the strongest grip on her own love life. But when it came to looking out for her best friend, Rachel was as loyal as they came.

Devin also knew that she wouldn't settle for a half-truth, at least not where Paris was concerned.

"No," he said, "I haven't told her."

"Then you do love her."

"Are you blind?" he asked, grinning. "Of course I love her."

"You should tell her."

Devin took Rachel's arm and led her off the dance floor. "Is Paris blind?"

"No, but she can be...nearsighted. Especially now." She waved her arm to encompass the house, the party. "And especially here."

"Why the sudden burst of matchmaking energy?"

Rachel tilted her head. "Honestly? Because I like you. I think you two are a match. And I think you're good for her, not one of these stuffy old dudes her father's drooling over."

"The child prodigy doesn't look stuffy."

Rachel's eyes widened. "Who?"

Devin pointed back to the dance floor, where Mr. Federal Prosecutor held Paris in his arms. "Him."

"Larry? Nah, he's okay, but he's not right for Paris. Besides, they've known each other since high school. If it was going to happen it already would have."

Devin looked again. Rachel was right. Paris was moving on the floor with Larry, but she wasn't *dancing* with him. Not the way she'd danced with Devin before. She didn't look bored, but neither did she look enraptured. As Larry spun her around, Paris looked in Devin's direction. When their eyes met, she smiled, and Devin went to mush.

"So you think I've still got a shot, here?"

"Oh, yeah. You're perfect for her," said Rachel. She stepped forward and crooked her finger, urging him to bend down. "But more than that," she whispered, "I figure if my goofy best friend who makes up fantasy men can find Mr. Right, then there's still hope for me."

Devin knew she was joking around, but he remembered what Paris had told him about Rachel's less-than-stellar track record with the opposite sex. He hooked a finger under her chin, tilting her head up and brushing a soft kiss across her temple. "Rach, there's definitely hope for you."

She blushed, a first as far as Devin could tell, then looked down. "Thanks," she whispered. When she looked back up, she smiled, and he thought her eyes might have been a little misty. "I told Paris she got the last good guy in New York. Looks like I was right."

He waved his hand to indicate the party. "Plenty of fish here in Texas."

She laughed. "A cowboy? No thanks. I'm a city girl, in case you hadn't noticed."

Devin was still chuckling at Rachel's last words as he

circled the dance floor in search of Paris. He thought
about what else Rachel had said, and decided that she
was right on target. Paris needed to know how he felt. She
needed to hear it out loud before she convinced herself
that she meant what she'd said about their three-week-
only deal.

He avoided getting sucked into another conversation
with a group of party guests by slipping behind the built-
in barbecue. As he reached the edge, he heard Paris's
voice. Devin eased back into the shadows.

"What I wanted to tell you, Daddy, is that I'm writing a
book," Paris said. Devin sucked in his breath. Was she
about to tell her father the truth?

"Well, good for you, sweetie. What kind of book? Non-
fiction?"

"No. Well, not exactly." Devin heard her take a breath.
"It's...oh, hell...I haven't written much of it yet, but it's
this saga. It starts in Ireland, and goes all the way through
the Civil War to the Depression."

"Well, that sounds fascinating. I'm surprised you have
time to write, traveling as much as you do."

"It's not easy."

"Have you thought about settling down?"

"I've thought about it," she said.

"Larry still adores you. Of course, Anson and Michael
are waiting in line." Devin felt a wave of dislike for Larry,
Anson and Michael. "You could do worse than a doctor
or a lawyer." The wave increased to tsunamic proportions.

"I know, Daddy. And Larry's a great guy..."

"Well, you're not getting any younger."

"Daddy," Paris said. "I'm barely thirty."

"Still. Are you seeing anyone seriously?"
Devin held his breath.

"No," Paris finally whispered, thrusting the knife into Devin's heart.

"No one," she said, twisting it.

Devin closed his eyes and fell against the rough brick surface. Anger, disappointment, despair battled for attention in his stomach. Disappointment won. He couldn't be angry at her, not really. She'd told him the ground rules on day one. He'd just been arrogant and foolish enough to think he could change her mind.

Fat chance, Devin. Look around you. You think Larry, Curly and Moe had to work their way through night school? Do you think their fathers had to pull cons to put food on the table?

He couldn't ignore the truth. She was a diamond, and he was coal.

Devin slammed the palm of his hand against the barbecue pit. Dammit, this wasn't a problem he could blame on his upbringing. Those guys weren't any better than him. He had to face that there were just some things that couldn't be had. Rachel was wrong. He wasn't the man for Paris. He'd fought bitterly to get an education, to make enough money to open his pubs, to have a good life. But none of that changed one important fact. Paris had only wanted him for three weeks. Three weeks of having her fantasy, of having Alexander, before she got on with her life.

And no matter how worthy he was, if she didn't think so, it was as good as over.

"AND NOW, the man of the hour, Mr. Montgomery Alexander," announced the bandleader.

Paris turned around to look for Devin, then winced when she saw him slip out from behind the brick grill and step to the podium. Had he heard everything? She took a step toward him. She needed to explain, to apologize. To say something.

Too late, of course. Devin stepped onto the platform and took the microphone.

"Mr. Alexander, Mr. Alexander!"

Paris couldn't see the man at the front of the crowd scrambling for attention, but from Devin's scowl, she guessed that something wasn't right.

"Mr. Alexander, isn't it true that there are going to be some revelations about you and your books? Very soon?"

Devin took a step backward, as if he'd just taken buckshot in the stomach. What was going on? Paris watched Devin skim the crowd until he found her. She raised her shoulders in a silent query.

Devin stared down the obnoxious little man. "Yes," he said, "some things will be revealed soon that I think will surprise my fans."

What revelations? What was he talking about?

"In the meantime, you'll just have to wait and see. Thank you for coming. Good night." He stepped off the platform.

Paris looked at her watch. He was supposed to speak for half an hour. Barely two minutes had passed since he hit the podium. Now he was striding through the crowd, heading in the opposite direction from her.

The second she cleared the side of the house, Paris broke into a run, planning to cut through the kitchen and head him off in the entry hall.

Rachel slammed breathless through the front door just as Paris reached the entry.

"Where is he?" Paris asked, winded. She had the feeling she already knew.

"Gone. He just pulled away in one of the hired cars."

Rachel took a breath and looked at Paris. "So what was that all about?"

Paris shook her head. "I don't know."

"Were we wrong about him? You don't think...?" Rachel trailed off, but Paris knew what she was considering.

"That he's planning to announce my secret? To blackmail me? No way. I don't think that. This revelation could be anything. Joshua's new partner, Vivian. The book deal. Maybe he's dyeing his hair back to blond. Anything."

Rachel nodded. "I know. I don't really believe it either. But what's going on? What's he talking about?"

Paris shook her head. "All I know is that Devin wouldn't do anything to hurt me."

"He left," Rachel pointed out.

Paris looked at the floor. "That's my fault. I hurt him first."

PATRICK SOMMERS slid a cup of coffee across the breakfast bar to Paris. "You've been moping about for four days, honey. Are you sure you won't tell me what's wrong? Did he fire you?"

Paris shook her head, sniffed and blew her nose.

She'd flat out lied to Devin. She'd promised him, *promised*, that she'd follow her heart, and then she'd gone and chickened out. She did love writing the Montgomery Alexander books.

And she loved Devin.

For days now, she'd been seeing him around every corner, hearing him every time the phone rang, running to the door every time a car drove up. And each time he wasn't there, her heart broke a little more.

Well, it stopped right now. She was going to do everything she could to get him back. Everything.

And Paris knew where she had to start.

"Daddy?"

He lowered his paper and looked at her. "Yes, sweetheart?"

"About that book I told you I was writing..."

When she'd told him the whole story, Paris had to admit she was impressed. Her father hadn't interrupted, and now he just sat there, quiet and pensive. And although quiet didn't necessarily mean all was well, from Paris's perspective, quiet was a heck of a lot better than ranting and raving.

"Daddy? Are you going to say anything?"

The judge clasped his hands and rested his chin on his steepled fingers. "I thought perhaps you were hiding something. I never dreamed you were writing those books. I thought you were in love with Mr. Alexander." He shook his head. "I mean, Devin."

"Yeah, well, I guess you get two for the price of one." She bit her lower lip and tried to read his face. "Are you okay with this?"

Judge Sommers stood up and poured himself a cup of coffee. He kept his back to Paris, staring out the window that overlooked the front drive. Paris shifted on her stool, anxious for him to say something, anything.

"Did I ever tell you why we named you Paris?" he finally asked, looking back over his shoulder at her.

Paris shook her head.

"We were dating, your mother and I. It was May. And your mother decided she wanted to see the Eiffel Tower. She was working in a secretarial pool, and I was in law school. She took her savings, and I took my schoolbook money, and we went to Paris. Just like that. That's where you were conceived. We were married the day we got back."

"No way. Who are you and what have you done with my father? That doesn't sound like you at all, Daddy."

He turned to face her, the tiniest smile playing at his mouth. "No, but it sounds a lot like your mother."

Paris's eyes welled. "Really? I always wanted to be like her. I thought you wanted me to. She's always seemed like this perfect person. The best hostess, the best wife, the best mother. Always doing the right thing, you know? The smart thing. Watching out for the family name. For you."

"She was all that and more." He took Paris's hand. "Your mother understood how important it is to sometimes just follow your heart."

"So you approve?"

"Approval is a big step for an old man at breakfast. Let's just say I understand. I can't argue too much with your mother's methods. After all, it got me you. And you're very much like her. I just want you to be secure." He smiled. "And happy. I want you to be happy."

She laughed, harshly, at her own stupidity. "Devin makes me happy. Why couldn't I have just told him that a couple of days ago?"

"You wouldn't have believed it yourself then."

Paris put down her mug. "Oh, Daddy. What am I going to do now?"

He stood behind her, stroking her hair like he had done so many times when she was a little girl needing comfort in the dark. But this wasn't the kind of problem a nightlight would solve. "Anything you have to."

The ringing phone interrupted her brooding.

Devin!

Paris lunged for it, scooping up the handset. "Devin?"

12

"PLEASE, CALL ME COURTLAND."

She regarded the old man perched in a wheelchair. He was wrapped in a flannel robe, an ashtray in front of him on the table, with an unopened package of cigarettes resting nearby. Courtland glanced down at the package often, as if it taunted him.

She'd rushed to the Houston airport only minutes after he'd called, taking only her purse and leaving her suitcases with her dad. She'd had to change planes twice—which meant enduring three takeoffs—before finally landing in New Jersey and taking a taxi to Mr. O'Malley's nursing home. But she'd endure just about anything for a chance to get Devin back. "I would have known you were Devin's father even if you hadn't told me. He looks just like you."

"Poor boy."

Paris laughed. "Not at all. And you know it."

"Once, maybe. But now I've got wrinkles and gray hair and nothing quite works the way it once did. Oh, the ladies around here don't complain much, but they're not exactly fresh off the farm themselves."

"You're extremely handsome. Sophisticated. Worldly. Sexy in a Paul Newman sort of way." She paused to make sure he was paying attention. He was, and she smiled at him. "And you can quit fishing now, because that's all the compliments you're going to lure out of me, even though each one is perfectly true."

"Spunky little thing. Of course you'd have to be for my son to fall for you."

Her heart leaped. Could what Courtland was saying really be true? And, more important, if it was, could she still get him back? "What makes you think he's fallen for me?"

"Television. My dear, the box sees all. I've watched you two on some of those interview shows. He looks at you that way."

"What way?"

"The same way you look at him."

"I'm in love with him." It felt good to say it. The more she said it, the stronger she felt. If she said it enough, she could get him back.

"I told him never to fall for a mark."

"I hired him. He's not blackmailing me." She grinned. "Well, he almost did. But he couldn't go through with it."

"I'm glad." Courtland looked out the window, but Paris didn't think he was seeing the trees and the clouds and the passersby. Courtland O'Malley was seeing the past and a little boy who'd beaten the odds. "I was afraid my debt drove him to turn his back on his own mind." He turned from the window to peer at her. "That's never good, you know. Doing something that's not true to your heart. Breaks the spirit."

She nodded. "Yeah. I just learned that one myself." She realized what else he had said. "Your debt?"

"I have a fondness for the ponies. My son's always managed to help me out. But this last time, I dealt with the wrong people. Should've known better. I've always been small-time. Got way in over my head, and they called in my marker."

"And Devin told them he'd cover it."

"I told him not to. After all, what can those fellows do to me in here?" he gestured around the cramped nursing home room. "My mind goes in and out. Half the time I don't even remember I owe the money."

"Devin's got his own code of honor. He couldn't let them hold that money over your head."

Courtland nodded. "I've never told him how proud I am of him not following my example. Oh sure, I taught him what to do, but that was because I was scared not to. What if he had failed at success? At least my kind of skills kept us from going hungry."

"But he hasn't failed," Paris said. "He's smart and funny and he must love you very much."

"Why isn't he with you?"

The question tore at her. "I made a mistake. I was following my head, and not my heart." A tear slid down her face, and she wiped it away. "And now I'm afraid I've lost him."

The old man crooked a finger, and Paris bent down to get closer. "If you want him, if you want love, you need to fight for it."

Paris nodded. "That's my plan."

"You're an idiot, boss," Jerry announced.

"Thanks, Jer. Your moral support is truly overwhelming." Devin lost his train of thought and had to start adding up the credit card receipts again. He'd been easily sidetracked for the past four days, and he knew the reason. Paris. No matter how hard he tried, he couldn't stop thinking about her. About her laugh, the feel of her body, her quirky sense of humor.

After overhearing her with her father, and then having one of Carmen's thugs make a not-so-subtle threat in Paris's own backyard, Devin had thought it was better for her if he left. But now? Now that every day was killing him, Devin was beginning to realize he was wrong.

He could give up a lot of things, but not Paris. His resolve had grown even stronger when he'd received the special delivery envelope that morning. Inside he'd found a check, neatly filled out in her precise handwriting, for six thousand dollars.

So she'd paid her debt, effectively severing her last tie to him. But that was an ending he just couldn't stomach. He needed her, and somehow he was going to get her back, or die trying.

"What's that old saying, Jerry? If you love something—"

"—hunt it down and kill it, boss."

Devin laughed. "Set it free. I think it's set it free."

Jerry shrugged. "Whatever. So?"

"The hell with that. If Larry, Curly and Moe want her that bad, they'll have to go after her through me, because I'm going back to Texas and I'm not leaving until that woman admits she loves me."

Jerry cast him a sideways look. "Ya got it bad, boss."

"Yeah, Jerry. I know."

Only after Devin stepped out into the Manhattan night, did he remember that it was three o'clock in the morning, and he wasn't going anywhere, much less hopping a plane to Texas. He considered going back in and helping Jerry, but the guy had been doing a fine job with the pub over the past three weeks, and Devin needed to get some rest if he was going to have the energy to wrestle Paris away from the three stooges.

He trudged the five blocks to his building and climbed three flights of stairs to his apartment. He'd left every light in the place on, he realized, as soon as he pushed open the door. No wonder his electric bill was always outrageous.

Then he saw her. Curled up on his battered sofa under an old quilt he'd rescued from a flea market.

He must have made a noise, or else she heard the Hallelujah Chorus playing in his head, because she stirred, then opened her eyes and squinted at him.

"Hey there," she said.

"Hi." Not poetry, but the best he could manage with his heart threatening to burst.

She pushed herself up to a sitting position. One of his old, ripped T-shirts barely covered her, giving him an enticing view of her thigh. Her hair was a mess, with wild curls going every which direction. Most of her makeup had rubbed off, except for the touch of mascara that was smudged under each eye.

She was the most beautiful thing he'd ever seen.

"What are you doing here?" he asked, almost afraid to hear the answer.

"Montgomery Alexander's not retiring. I told my dad. I told him everything." She smiled. "There wasn't exactly gunfire. Maybe a few stray shots, but overall it went well." She twirled a strand of hair around her finger, and he couldn't help but grin. "I always thought that I wanted a certain kind of man and that I wanted to write a certain type of book. I thought that if I got that man, that life, then I could be happy."

Devin tried not to anticipate where Paris was going. He was terrified of being wrong. Terrified she'd flown all the way here simply to say thanks for playing the role, have a nice life, and by the way, thanks for making the mob notice me and my little scheme.

He swallowed. "What are you saying?"

"That I never knew what I wanted. But I do now. The

man I want can dance on the beach or in a ballroom. He can make love to me with a passion so intense it ignites my soul. He's suave, yet funny. He works hard, but he knows how to play. He loves adventure, but a perfect Sunday morning is reading the paper in bed. And most of all, he loves me." She stared at him with an intensity that cut to his core. "I love you, Devin. You. And I'm sorry I didn't say it before."

Devin exhaled, relieved, but still wary. "I'm not Alexander."

"I don't want Alexander. Alexander doesn't even exist." She stood up. "I don't want an Alexander, or an accountant or a social climber." She took a step closer. "I want you. I want the man who charmed me and teased me. I want the man who's so fiercely loyal to his family that he's willing to cover a gambling debt that's not even his own."

"You talked with my dad."

"He's a sweetheart. He told me to fight for you." She grinned. "And he gave me his key to your apartment."

He pulled her to him. "Remind me to thank him," he whispered, bending down to claim her mouth, to claim her. This was the woman for him, and nothing could come between them.

Except...

He gently broke the kiss, pulling away to look down at her face. He saw confusion in her eyes.

"What is it?" she asked.

"It's not just about you and me. Alexander is part of this."

"No, he—"

"They'll never leave us alone," he insisted.

She shook her head. "We can pay off your dad's debt."

He stepped back from her, gently stepping away from

her outstretched hand urging him back to her. He ran his hands through his hair, dreading telling her. But she had to know.

When he looked back at her, she was smiling.

"What?"

"I like your hair blond. It's sexy."

"Paris, if we don't pay them, they're going to reveal that Alexander doesn't exist."

He watched her brow furrow and her mouth curl into a small, adorable frown. "The men in Vegas?" she asked.

He nodded.

"The press conference," she said. "That guy was making a threat, and you were setting it up so that I could introduce me. It wasn't the new character or the book deal or anything else you were thinking about."

"If you don't go public that you're the real author, then you'll be under their thumb forever." He fixed his gaze upon her. "I can't live with knowing I brought that on you."

"Did you like being Alexander?"

"That's not the issue."

She nodded furiously. "Oh, yes. It's exactly the issue. I'm without an Alexander. He can go back into seclusion, of course. But if you enjoyed it, he wouldn't have to."

"I loved it," he admitted, then laughed. "Maybe I am my father's son."

She laughed. "And maybe you're my soul mate. After all, I guess I'm Alexander, too."

"Soul mates. I like the sound of that."

"Can you do it? Even just part-time? Can you keep being Alexander and still manage your pub?"

Of course he could, but that wasn't the point. "Paris, these men—"

"Can you?" she interrupted.

"Jerry's been managing the pub here, and doing a great job. We close next week on the Boston pub, and I've got a couple of people in line to run it. I'll need to spend some time up there getting it off the ground, supervising the finish-out, but nothing too extensive. I'd actually like not to have to do the day-to-day stuff. I'm more interested in opening a few more." He smiled at her. "I thought Texas might be a good venue."

"Well, see?"

No, he didn't see. "All I know is that if Alexander becomes a recluse again, maybe these thugs will forget about you. If I'm out there front and center, they'll hound us for life."

"I'm not letting these men come between us. And I'm not letting them dictate what I do with my life or my books." She turned to face him, her eyes defiant. "It took me a long time to realize that I can't even do that for my dad. Not and be happy. I certainly won't do it for some two-bit thugs who don't have anything better to do than threaten invalid old men and helpless authors."

"You're hardly helpless," he said, feeling proud as he watched her stand straight and determined. She was one gutsy woman.

"Well, I fudged a little on that part."

"Do you have any ideas?"

She shook her head. "No. You?"

Neither did he. He studied the floor for a while, looking for a brilliant plan buried in the polished wood. Nothing.

But then…

He looked up, and she was staring at him, her eyes bright.

"I've got an idea," they said together, then laughed.

THE MAN CALLED Carmen gave Paris the creeps, but the one called Bull outright scared her. A jagged scar cut across his cheek, his dark eyes cold.

For a moment, she wished she had a drink, but it was early in the morning and the pub was technically closed. She looked around the room at the empty tables. Just her and Devin and the creepazoid twins.

She squeezed Devin's hand under the table and he squeezed back. His touch reassured her. She took a breath. Show time.

"You wanted me to bring her, and I did. But you'll have to convince her," Devin said. He crossed his arms over his chest and leaned back in the booth.

"I really don't understand. What is it you gentlemen need to speak to me about?" she asked, resisting the urge to spit in their faces.

Carmen leered, revealing one gold tooth. "That's a good question, Miss Sommers. You see we're in the protection business. We know your little secret. And we can make certain that nobody else finds out."

"Well, that's interesting," she said, leaning across the table and coming even closer to the disgusting beasts. "But I don't really understand how it works."

For the next fifteen minutes, Carmen proceeded to explain, in intricate detail, why his protection service was so effective, along with the amount of that pesky monthly charge that ensured the protection went on and on.

"So, what do you think, Paris? Have you heard enough?" Devin asked.

She replayed the conversation back in her mind. Not the cleanest evidence in the world, but it would do.

Paris flashed her best smile at Carmen and Bull. "Yes. Yes, I think I've heard everything I need to."

Devin lifted his arm and rapped on the wall behind him. "Got that, guys?"

"Loud and clear," came the muffled response, and Paris couldn't help but smile when she saw the expression on Carmen's and Bull's faces.

When the two thugs were led away in cuffs amidst a flurry of activity Paris felt as though she was in one of her novels. She wanted to applaud, but quelled the urge. Instead, she kissed Devin.

"Thank you."

Devin shook his head. "Don't thank me. Your father's the one who got Larry to come out here, and Larry's the one who got the local cops involved."

"I'm not the one who thought of calling my father."

"There's no guarantee that tape will stop them or even end anyone up in jail. The wheels of justice don't exactly spin at a fast clip. You should know. But this way, harassing us is a lot less appealing."

"I know. And blackmailing us would be pointless after we run through Plan B, so I'd say we're all set."

"Did you call Rachel?"

Paris nodded. "Everything's ready. Are you?"

"Ready to spend the rest of my life with you? Oh, yeah. I'm ready."

Paris laughed. "Ready for a press conference?"

Devin shrugged. "That, too." He smiled at her, but made no move to walk to the door.

"What is it?"

"Have I told you today that I love you?"

She smiled. "Yeah. But you can tell me again."

"I love you."

Paris stretched her arms around his neck and kissed him, this man of her dreams who had literally made her fantasies come true. "I love you, too."

Epilogue

HOUSTON, TEXAS—Bestselling author Devin O'Malley married his manager and recent co-author Paris Sommers yesterday. O'Malley is better known as Montgomery Alexander, the reclusive author of a popular series of espionage thrillers. O'Malley surprised Alexander's fans six months ago by announcing at a press conference that Alexander was O'Malley's pseudonym.

Even more surprising was the announcement that, for future books, Montgomery Alexander will be the pen name for the dual effort of Sommers and O'Malley. The couple revealed that the next Joshua Malloy book will team the superspy with a female partner, Vivian Jones, promising that the leather-clad, stiletto-wielding heroine will keep Malloy, and his fans, wanting more.

The ceremony was held in the bride's family home in River Oaks. The bride's father, Judge Patrick Sommers, performed the nuptials.

Devin tossed the paper on the floor and pulled his naked bride next to him. He liked the sound of that. *Bride.*

"You tired?"

She didn't answer, just eased on top of him, moving her body over his until he was just as aroused as he'd been less than an hour before. And an hour before that.

She kissed the top of his ear. "What did you have in mind?"

"Research," he said.

"More research?" she teased.

"Hey, Malloy's never had a female partner before. If you're going to write these scenes, you need to make sure you've done all the prep work."

"Mmm, that's very thoughtful."

"Well, since you're doing all the writing and I'm just a pretty face, I thought it only fair to do my part."

She sat up, straddling his waist and arching her back as he reached up to stroke her breasts with one hand, teasing and tempting her. His Paris, his wife.

"Eventually," she said, her voice ragged, "I'm going to have to stop researching and start writing."

He chuckled, but didn't stop. "All in good time, my dear. All in good time."

Temptation

A spicy hot love story

BLAZE

Available in February 2000

IN TOO DEEP

by
Lori Foster
(Temptation #770)

Charlotte (Charlie) Jones was used to fighting for what
she wanted, and she wanted Harry Lonigan—big-time!
But the sexy P.I. was doing his best to deny the steamy
attraction between them. Charlie was the daughter of
his best friend and father figure so, to his mind, she
was off-limits. But as he worked with Charlie on
an embezzling case, Charlie worked on him.
Before he knew it, Harry was in too deep.

BLAZE! Red-hot reads from Temptation!

Available at your favorite retail outlet.

HARLEQUIN®
Makes any time special ™

Visit us at www.romance.net

HTBL300

Coming in February 2000

WHO'S AFRAID OF A BIG BAD WOLFE?

Not the special ladies who tame the remaining
Wolfe brothers in these sensuous love stories by
beloved author **Joan Hohl.**

Available February 2000 at your favorite retail outlet.

Where love comes alive™

Come escape with Harlequin's new

Series Sampler

Four great full-length Harlequin novels bound together in one fabulous volume and at an unbelievable price.

Be transported back in time with a Harlequin Historical® novel, get caught up in a mystery with Intrigue®, be tempted by a hot, sizzling romance with Harlequin Temptation®, or just enjoy a down-home all-American read with American Romance®.

You won't be able to put this collection down!

On sale February 2000 at your favorite retail outlet.

HARLEQUIN®
Makes any time special ™

Temptation

BLAZE

It's hot...and it's out of control!

Pick up a **Blaze** for an experience you'll never forget. It's the bold, provocative and ultrasexy read that is sure to leave you breathless!

Join some of your favorite authors, such as Lori Foster and Vicki Lewis Thompson, for stories filled with passion and seduction.

Temptation brings you a brand-new **Blaze** every month.

Look for it at your favorite retail outlet.